Moon Diamonds

A Siamese Cat Story

By

Madeleine Purslow

With love to Jules, Anna, Fran and all my other friends at Siamese Lovers.

With thanks to Rob and to Shelley for their assistance.

The Legend

When the great Moon Goddess created Siamese cats, she wanted them to be as magnificent as possible. So that everyone would look at them and see her own radiance reflected in their beauty.

She made their bodies lithe and svelte, their tails long and elegant and their fur as pale as the moon. Then she touched their noses, ears, tails and paws, and gave them their beautiful coloured points, so that they would be distinct from all other cats.

Finally she bestowed her greatest gift of all upon them. She gave them blue moon diamonds for their eyes, as a sign of her unceasing love for them.

But when she had finished, she surveyed her wonderful children and realized that she had in fact created perfection. And then she wept, for she knew that no perfect creature is allowed to live on the earth.

Days passed as the great Moon Goddess pondered her dilemma. How could she bear to change anything about these glorious creatures? How could she bear to give them an imperfection? And then finally, she knew.

She would give them a flaw that no one would ever be able to see. She gave them their harsh voices……..

Chapter One

Monica had laughed it off too many times. She was beginning to run out of excuses. At first there had been the odd little slip now and again-someone's name, the title of a play, or a place. Nothing too terrible. She liked to call it her "Moth Brain", bits and pieces fluttering and flitting away as she tried to catch them.

Everyone knew that feeling, being at a party and being introduced to someone and then instantly forgetting their name. She had a busy brain stuffed full of words, directions, and cues, things were bound to leak out. And anyway, as soon as the prompt stepped in she was away again, as word perfect as ever.

But this play *Like Lemon Drops,* was different. People had started to become irritable with her, implying she hadn't learned her script properly, or that she'd had one too many in the bar at lunch. Either way, it wasn't a comfortable place to be and she was getting worried.

That afternoon she had forgotten her lines six times! Six! This was the woman who had learned *Nerissa* in one weekend when the leading lady and her understudy had disappeared on a bender together.

As a student, she remembered, she had felt quite sorry for one older actress who had seemed to be losing her hearing. It had been embarrassing watching her struggle. But Monica was young then and it never occurred to her that she would have to deal with such things. Young people don't get old, do they?

She had expected "The Sag," of course. Nearly all actresses go through it, that part in your life when you are just a little too old for the ingénue, and much too young for character parts. Old bags or babies ……and nothing in the middle, except for the odd mistress or dowdy house wife now and then.

Monica had survived it all but now her brain was letting her down. No moths in her brain any more, they had done their work and left behind huge gaping holes where the wind whistled through. A second before she was due to speak she knew the line, the minute she opened her mouth they simply fell away, dropped completely out of her head.

Trevor was as calm as ever about it, putting it down to anxiety. "It's a vicious circle, Mon. The more you think about it, the more it will happen." She didn't think about it but huge gaps still suddenly appeared and like buildings in an earthquake her lines fell through the cracks.

As she sat brooding over her afternoon from hell, a dark mood engulfed her. It was a combination of tiredness and self-pity, and it made her feel worthless. She was letting everyone down. They were all pretending to be understanding, of course but she knew she was a burden. She was the one that stopped the flow and held everyone up.

She glanced up at her publicity shot, jammed in the frame of her mirror. She didn't look bad for her age, she could have years left in her yet. This was so unfair.

There was a soft knock on her door and Christian let himself in.

"Monique, are you okay?"

"Yes, yes, just tired, you know?"

She dragged a brush though her grey bob and met his eyes in the mirror. It seemed more comfortable than actually turning to face him.

"It's just, you seemed a little........off your game. Not quite top drawer, as it were."

Christian's obsequious manner irritated her. Why didn't he just come out and say it. He was the director after all. Why not just tell her? *You're not good enough, Monique. You're too old.* Instead of this pussy footing around.

She fixed him with one of her Eileen Atkins withering looks.

"No, Christian, I wasn't top drawer, as you put it. I wasn't even middle drawer. I was the bottom drawer, the one that has come off its runners. That was what I was, Christian!"

Her director flinched. "Look, Monique, just go over your lines tonight, get some rest and we'll do it all again tomorrow, hmmm?"

"Tomorrow is another day," she said, snatching up her bag and reaching for her mac. She marched quickly along the plush red theatre corridor and out into the real world.

On her drive home, she gnawed away at the day, going over and over her mistakes, trying not to remember that moment when she had emerged from the velvety womb of the theatre and into the harsh, dark light of the winter afternoon. The moment when she wondered, she might have to give it all up.

Sitting at the traffic lights watching other people heading home from their mundane little jobs, she realized that she had no idea what that felt like, to go to work every day and do the same thing. Her world had been so full of variety and she couldn't imagine not being part of it any more. All that world carrying on, but without her: not having the right to go back stage, not having the next production to look forward to, no applause. What would she do? Acting was all she had ever done, all she had ever wanted to do. She didn't want it to end like this, she wanted to go on until she dropped. Was she really, seriously thinking of leaving the profession?

When she pulled up on the drive she could see the light was on in Trevor's office. He would be in there, learning his lines, Mahler blasting away. He had just got a role in *Mrs Brown* at The Lyric and he was relishing the idea. Men always got such wonderful parts, they **could** go on forever.

Tonight was not the night to talk to him about her dark thoughts. He would just put it down to tiredness and infuriate her even more. He had been making excuses for her for months now, and whether he believed them himself or was just in denial, she wasn't sure. But she didn't want reassurances tonight, however well meant. She just wanted to wallow and think.

At times like this she missed Claudette, who would have told her the truth and together they would have decided what to do. *There is always an answer.* But now she had to find that answer alone.

She would have a shower, go through the script again with a glass of scotch in her hand and pray that she would suddenly be cured in the morning, that magically her memory would go back to normal so there would be no decision to make.

As she let herself in quietly, she could hear Trevor reading aloud from his script behind the closed door of his study. He wouldn't have noticed the time, he wouldn't be expecting her back, so she slipped off her shoes and padded into the lounge. She opened the door and turned on the light. Immediately she was met by a strange sleepy whine, as her Siamese opened her dainty pink mouth and let out a huge yawn.

Hopping lightly down from the armchair, Theodosia stretched out her front legs and flexed her claws. Trotting across the carpet she let her back legs elongate behind her for a moment, tensing and then releasing them to catch up with the rest of her body. This languorous display immediately made Monica feel even more tired than she already was.

"Hello, sweetheart," she said. "Is Daddy being boring again and not paying you any attention? Did he remember to feed you? Let's go and look in your bowl."

Theodosia had been a tiny, bossy little thing when she had arrived ten years ago. She had been a present from Monica's dear friend Clive, at Stratford, and they had decided between them to name her Theda, in honour of the silent screen goddess Theda Bara. But after a few months of people calling her Freda, Monica had changed it. No cat of hers was going to have such a working class name.

Theodosia had never been a kitten, she came into the world fully grown. Had she been human, her first words would have been, "Right! I'll soon sort this lot out." No kittenish games for her - she got to work straight away on organising the household to her liking. A delicate lilac point with huge cornflower blue eyes, she looked the very picture of sweetness, but inside that velvet paw were claws of steel.

In the kitchen her bowl was half full. The food had not been entirely to Madame Theodosia's liking, that much was clear. Going to the fridge, closely supervised by her cat, Monica pulled a piece of smoked salmon from its tray and dropped it onto the floor.

"There you are, darling. Now, Mummy is going in the shower and then up to bed to learn her hateful script."

Before Monica reached the kitchen door, the salmon had vanished and Theodosia was twinkling along at her heels. "I'm going in the wet stuff now. You won't like it, you know you won't."

The two climbed the stairs together, the Siamese taking two stairs at once and Monica plodding behind. She felt weary to the bone. It was as though God had devised a particularly evil torture for her, one that would hurt her most. An actress who couldn't remember her lines? That wasn't an actress at all, was it?

When Monica turned to go into the bathroom, Theodosia skidded to a halt. "Told you," said Monica, gently closing the door behind her.

When she woke the next morning with the pages of her script still lying on top of the duvet, Monica felt fine, or at least for an instant she did. Watery winter sun was shining through the blinds and Trevor was gently snoring beside her. Everything was as it usually was, but then she remembered the nightmarish day before: the panic of forgetting her lines, the fear of having to stop doing what she loved. Even now, despite all the reading and re-reading she had done last night, she couldn't remember one single line of the script. There was just a horrible blank. She wanted to go back to sleep and escape it all, but she knew there could be no running away. She had to get up and go to rehearsal. Her stomach contracted at the thought and she immediately felt sick. This was going to be a long day.

At breakfast, she chose not to share her fears with Trevor. He was full of his new role. If he hadn't been her dear, lovely husband she would have said that he was absorbed by his own greatness. It wasn't his fault of course, it was how actors got sometimes. The world could be exploding around them and they wouldn't notice or care as long as they got their character right. And Trevor was in love with his new Scottish character.

She put the dishes into the sink for Patty to do when she got in, and went upstairs to find some clothes that made her feel like an actress. She may as well dress the part while she still could.

Chapter Two

Monica paused for a moment outside the theatre. She was determined to look fabulous: high heels (ridiculous for rehearsals), straight leg black jeans, a Jacquard green top and a huge sage scarf swept around her neck. She had her costume, now all she had to do was perform.

She lifted her head and strode in through the stage door. She wasn't going to let anyone see just how terrified she was, this old girl was not going quietly. Her mother had always told her, "There is always an answer." And today she would give them that answer.

Once inside the warm, musty, welcoming theatre, she began to relax a little. This is where she belonged. She turned left into the ladies and checked her appearance once more. Yes, she'd do. Looking down at her script she said aloud, "A girl doesn't read this sort of thing without her lipstick." A quick dab of gloss and a flick of her hair and she was ready.

She walked determinedly towards the other actors who were all congregating backstage, clutching their take out coffees like their lives depended on it. A few nodded or flicked a hand in welcome. Perhaps they had been talking about her? After yesterday she wouldn't have blamed them, but that was over. Today was another day and today, she would be back on top form, or in that bloody drawer Christian was so fond of talking about.

After a few tense moments their director arrived, messenger bag slung over one shoulder and mobile jammed to his ear.

"Right!" he said, ending his call. "So, three weeks to the Tech, and we all have to up our games a little. I want to see plenty of energy out there and can we please try to get the blocking spot on today? You were wandering around like lost sheep yesterday. Monique, are you feeling better?"

Monica was mortified. How dare he single her out like that in front of the others. She smiled confidently and said, "I'm fine. Raring to go, actually."

"Good, then let's go from Scene Three. The one we had so much trouble with yesterday. Chop, chop, everyone, positions."

Monica was in Scene Three. In fact she had quite a bit to do. *Stay calm*, she told herself, *just stay calm and it'll all flow*.

"So, good, good, everyone. Now remember these are normal working class people, totally out of their depth. So let's pick it up from Clare's line, *Don't we have to dress up and that*? And……"

"Don't we have to dress up and that, Dad?"

"No, not if we don't want to."

"You will be dressing up, Graham! I'm not having you show us up."

"What's wrong with being ourselves?"

And then…… SILENCE. Monica knew she was supposed to be giving a speech about not wanting to be herself, wanting to be someone else for just a little while, but it had fallen through the cracks, just drifted away into the ether.

The other actors shifted uncomfortably and took sly sidelong looks at her, one of them even audibly sighed. *Think, Monica, think!* she told herself. *What's the line, what does Maureen say? Oh, for God's sake.* It just wouldn't come, there was an absolute blank.

"Sorry, sorry everyone," she said. "I know I'm making a shitty mess of this, please just bear with me." Monica grabbed her script and started to frantically flick through the pages. The more anxious she felt, the less she could see. "Hang on, hang on. With you in a minute."

Christian stepped in. Taking the script from her he said, "Okay guys, give us a moment would you?" Then, taking Monica's hand he steered her down from the stage and into the front row of seats.

Monica was shaking by now and was glad to have the security of a chair beneath her.

"Monique, what's going on? Have you learned any of your scenes?"

Running a hand through her hair, Monica wondered how to explain without sounding like she was losing her mind. After a moment she said, "The truth is, Christian, I just can't remember the bloody words. I learn them and they just don't stick any more. Oh God, this is so awful. I don't know what's happening to me?"

The director took her hand in his. "Look, Monique, you know I love you, and I want you to be in my play, but if there is something bothering you we need to get it sorted out."

"No, honestly I'm fine. I've just got myself into a stupid state, that's all. Let's have another go. I'll just check the script and…." As she reached over to take the script from Christian's hand, he held onto it.

"No, Monique, go home and get some rest. We can work around you for a few days. But look, you need to get yourself checked out. Now, off you go."

Monica rose unsteadily. "If you insist, Christian, but I feel so pathetic. I've never let anyone down before."

"And you're not now, just go. We'll speak soon." He stood and kissed her lightly on the cheek.

As she made her way slowly out of the auditorium, tears began to sting her eyes. Now it was real, she couldn't gloss over it any more. For a while now, she had not felt like herself, not since Claudette had passed. It was almost as though she had been staring out at the world through someone else's eyes, as though she was in there somewhere but a long way back. Of course, she had carried on as normal, she was an actress, that's what they did. If you act okay, you become okay. In the past the stage had always been her saviour, her refuge from real life. But this time she just felt long and stretched, grey and tired.

She knew of course, that she had been lucky to have her marvellous, magical mother for so long,

15

but when someone so bright and alive as Claudette leaves the world it was hard to accept that you would never see them again. They had happily shared their lives and even their home but now it was over. Slowly she had been coming to terms with it, but now her memory was failing and it felt like the final straw. She was officially an orphan and about to go ga ga.

Of course Christian probably thought she had one of those old people's things, dementia or whatever, but she was pretty sure that whatever was happening to her, it was not that. She knew what year it was, who the prime minister was, all those ridiculous things they asked one in these situations. It was just certain things that she couldn't remember, like the top layer of her memory was failing.

She had first noticed it a few months ago, and it was happening more and more. What she needed was a rest. It was nonsense to think about giving up the stage, all she needed was a little time to get herself straight. *Get yourself checked out* - indeed. Actors didn't need medics or shrinks, they just needed to work and so, after a break she'd be fine, back and firing on all cylinders again.

But now she was going home, home to see her beautiful lilac faced Theodosia, who loved her whatever she did and whatever she looked like. And whatever she could or couldn't remember.

Chapter Three

As Monica drove home, she felt overwhelmed by a huge wave of bleak tiredness. She had been up less than four hours but the experience at the theatre had left her feeling exhausted. She knew Trevor had gone to London and so she decided to do something she had never done in her life. Go back to bed.

Going back to bed was unheard of when she was growing up. As a teenager if she tried to sleep late, Claudette would appear on the landing crashing about with the vacuum cleaner and singing loudly in French. Lying in bed was lazy, it was a waste of the day and not to be tolerated. A lesson that had always served Monica well. Until now that was. Now she felt that it was all she wanted to do, just slip into bed, and drift away to oblivion for a while. She would take Theodosia with her of course. She was twelve now and was always ready to share a snooze.

Theodosia would burrow down under the sheets, nestle into Monica's side and make the endearing little snoring sounds that made her muzzle blow out in tiny little puffs of air. It was the most restful, relaxing sound imaginable and when Trevor was away, they slept blissfully together. That was what she wanted now, to be asleep with Theodosia.

When she finally turned into the drive, she realized her mistake. Patty would still be there.

Annoying, garrulous, vacuous Patty, with her endless stories and her flat northern vowels.

Patty was an excellent cleaner and Theodosia loved her, but for Monica's part, she tried to avoid her. The only time Monica had voluntarily spent time in her company was when she was playing the part of a Yorkshire farmer's wife, and then she had studied Patty's speech pattern assiduously. It had been a frustrating experience and one she was not in a hurry to repeat.

But there was nothing she could do about it now. Patty was there and she would just have to deal with it. Putting on her best carefree face, she got out of the car and bounded up the drive. Even before she opened the front door she could hear Patty chatting away. Fortunately, Theodosia was a good listener.

"Well, everybody knew she were two bob short of a shilling," Patty droned. "But when she told us her antie used to keep pet mice in a biscuit tin, well we didn't know where to put ourselves. Mice! Can you believe it?"

Her diatribe was cut short by Monica poking her head round the kitchen door and saying, "Patty, hello. I've just come back to go over part of my script. You just pretend I'm not here."

The cleaner paused, mop in hand and pursed her lips in consideration.

"Well, you say pretend you aren't here, but I know now, don't I? That you're here. You should have just got on with it and said nowt." She went back to mopping.

"Well, yes I'm sorry. I didn't want you to think I was an intruder or anything."

"I doubt I'd have thought that."

"No," thought Monica, *"you wouldn't have the imagination, would you? "* But she said, "Well, anyway I'll stay out of your way. Come on, Theodosia. Come and see Mummy."

The cat jumped down from the kitchen chair where she had been watching the hypnotic swish of Patty's mop, and having shaken her lilac paws as she crossed the damp floor, she then rubbed herself against Monica's legs. But once the greeting was over she returned to her seat and continued to watch the cleaner.

"Looks like you've lost your friend, I'd say," pointed out Patty. "Me and Thea-dosia will be fine. Just you get on with what you've got to do and don't worry about us."

As Monica left the room, Theodosia blinked her deep blue blink and settled herself down to listen to more of Patty's endless tales.

Deflated Monica made her way up the stairs, even her beautiful girl had let her down. She stood for a moment looking out of the tall landing window across the wintery dun coloured fields. Trevor and she had lived in the village for seven years now, and yet she still felt like an outsider. It was a beautiful spot but she felt no real connection with it. The Stonehouse was just their base. Well, maybe over the next few days she would have time to investigate a little more. It was going to be tough, slowing down, but somehow she had to make it work.

She went into the bedroom and began to take off her clothes. They felt faintly silly now, the high heeled boots and tight jeans. For once she hadn't carried off the role. In just her underwear she climbed into the bed and prepared for sleep.

At first her mind ran over and over the awfulness of that morning and the potential hopelessness of her future. She felt close to tears. She missed her mother so much and this was the first real crisis she had had to face without her. If only she could have picked the phone up and talked to her, just one more time, just to tell her what had happened, just to hear her fierce, French voice again.

As tears welled under her closed eyelids, she hear a squeak as the bedroom door opened. *God!* She thought. *I should have told nosey Patty that I didn't want to be disturbed.* A few moments later something softly landed at the bottom of the bed and then, like a tank, she felt Theodosia roll right over her, paws jabbing her side as she came. Whiskers brushed against Monica's cheek and a probing lilac foot pawed at the sheet.

"Bree-ow!" she said.

The pawing continued until Monica lifted the sheet and allowed her to wander down the bed before eventually settling with an elongated purr of satisfaction against Monica's warm back.

Siamese cats, a final and lasting gift of comfort from Claudette. Monica had never been without a Siamese, their angular heads and large bat like ears

20

were as familiar to her as her own face. She sometimes forgot that people found them a little strange, alarming even, with that penetrating deep blue gaze and odd vocalisations.

Every now and again she would see what they saw, a peculiar, exotic creature, as unearthly as a unicorn, with knowing eyes and slender lithe bodies. But mostly they were her friends, a constant in her life, a part of her before she was even born.

The first cat she could remember clearly was Pasquale, a big blue point, with prominent fangs, and a penchant for ice cream. Monica and he had grown up together. He was the first cat her mother had after coming to live in England. Later there had been Simone, who was a huntress and had a wildness about her; when she and Pasquale were together, Monica's mother was at her happiest.

As they shook their heads, and made sharp snapping noises with their oversized ears, Claudette would smile indulgently and say,

"Monique, listen, we are surrounded by flocks of ears."

Claudette doted on her cats and would often wander about with one of them draped about her neck like a scarf, as though it were perfectly normal. But in fact there was very little that was normal about Claudette. She had married Monica's dashing soldier father, Eric in a romantic whirl during the last days of the war.

The mayor had married them in his crumbling bombed town hall, or at least that was how Claudette liked to tell it. Monica was never sure.

Her mother was never one to let the truth get in the way of a good dramatic story. In a good many ways Monica's mother was an enigma. For instance, why did she stay with Eric? Was he a safe haven after the desperation and romance of the war? They must soon have found that they had nothing really in common, and yet they endured. They disagreed about almost everything, including the name of their own daughter. Claudette always called her Monique, while her father registered her as good old plain Monica. Monique was to become her stage name much to the delight of her mother.

Eric and Claudette shared a house, and a daughter, but very little else. Monica's father was taciturn and straight forward and sensible to his very bones. Unexpected or spontaneous were not in his vocabulary. Whereas her mother was a strange mercurial whimsical being, always having new ideas and pursuing odd crazes and fancies.

As a child Monica would often go to school only to return later in the day to find that all the furniture had been completely rearranged, and not just on the first floor, but all over the house. How her tiny bird like mother achieved this was never clear, but pure willpower was one of Claudette's strongest points. She may have looked frail but she had a will of iron.

One of the first things she did when she got to England, was to go in search of a Siamese cat. When most newly married women would have been worrying about running a home and planning a family, Claudette's priority was her cat. And a Siamese one at that. Perhaps, Monica thought, the Siamese reminded her of herself? Foreign, exotic, far from home and struggling with the repressive English society.

But she somehow managed to find one, and according to Eric, pay and exorbitant price for him. Pasquale arrived, and at least two years later Monica came along. Her mother's priorities were clear. She used to say that she didn't feel herself with a Siamese.

And now she had passed that love onto Monica. She too could not imagine life without a Siamese. Although she had to admit that her job was not ideal for pet ownership, she had always had Claudette there to help.

As she lay in bed that winter afternoon, with Theodosia snoring delicately at her back, Monica felt that while she had a Siamese, she would always have a little piece of Claudette's soul. Gently the two of them drifted off into a serene sleep.

Chapter Four

When Monica woke, she wasn't sure where she was. It wasn't unusual for her, years of touring had meant that she often didn't recognise her surroundings at first, but this was slightly different. Not only did she not know where she was, she wasn't sure of the time or even the day.

Theodosia squeaked her disapproval as Monica started to move. Something had woken her, and she wasn't sure what.

"Mrs P, I'll leave you to it, then." It was Patty, calling to her from the landing. Suddenly Monica remembered, she was home, sleeping in the day! Frantically she shot out of bed and grabbed her robe. She didn't want her cleaner to catch her in bed. Raking her hands through her hair she tried to compose herself.

"Okay, thanks. Might see you in the morning, then. I'm working from home for a few days," she shouted, in a remarkably steady voice.

Thankfully Patty decided not to venture into the bedroom and Monica heard her heavy footsteps heading downstairs.

"Just as you like. Be working in the bedroom again, will ya?" she called back.

"Mmmm, I don't know, possibly. I won't get in your way."

There was no reply and the front door slammed shut. Monica sat on the side of the bed. What did Patty mean, *working in the bedroom?* Did she know? Had she been in and seen her sleeping? Angrily she got up from the bed and went towards the shower. A querulous meow from under the duvet reminded her of Theodosia's presence and a moment later a yawning lilac face popped out.

"Yow!" she said "Yow!"

Monica went back and stoked her companion's downy head.

"I'm sorry, sweetheart. Did I wake you up? Never mind, we will have all day together tomorrow. I'm just having a little holiday."

The cat stretched and settled back down with one front paw delicately placed over the other, blissfully unaware of just how wretched Monica was feeling. *A little holiday?* It was the last thing she wanted, but somehow she would have to make the best of it.

It was now around one o'clock and the whole morning had simply drifted away. Suddenly feeling very decadent Monica took a long shower, painted her toe nails and felt every inch the lady of leisure. Now she was sitting in the lounge, with Theodosia curled up on her lap, like a silvery fur hat. This wouldn't be so bad, she told herself. She hadn't had a break in years. Like most actresses, if there was work offered to her, she had always taken it. So now it was time for her to go easy on herself, to be lazy. And why not? Last year had been horrendous, a string of lousy jobs and then her mother passing away at Christmas before last. Maybe it was time to indulge herself a little. Tomorrow she would go into

25

the village, wander around the shops, chat to people, maybe have a coffee in Caraway's tea shop. Just follow her nose and see where it led her. Then, after a few days R and R, she would ring...... erm. And there it was, the blank space where a name should have been... She would ring.... No, it was gone. What was his bloody name? The director. Oh, God this was annoying. She could see his little ferrety face in her mind's eye, but his name had escaped through one of her brain holes.

Feeling suddenly hot, she grabbed her mobile. She needed to talk to Trevor, just to hear his calm tones. He would probably be in rehearsal, but she could leave a message, she knew he checked regularly in case any work came in.

As the phone clicked to voice mail, Monica realized that she had no idea what she was going to say. She always knew what to say, always! She was one of those people who just picked the phone up and got on with it, no planning. But this time she was blank. She ended the call without speaking.

Lifting Theodosia to her face, she sniffed in the warm comforting scent of her fur and felt her muscular little body next to hers. Alarmed at being disturbed the cat wriggled from her grasp and jumped down. With a short sharp croak of annoyance she made her way out of the room, abandoning Monica to her dark thoughts.

For a while she just sat. The house seemed utterly silent. Theodosia had gone up to find some peace in one of the bedrooms and Monica was alone. Alone on a glum winter afternoon, wondering what to do with herself.

She really felt as though she should be doing something mind improving, but it all seemed like too much effort, so instead she switched on the television. It was quite a foreign concept to her. Being in the entertainment business meant that she very rarely saw any of it. All the "big shows" people talked about were a complete mystery to her. She knew people complained a lot about it, and on one memorable occasion she had heard Patty saying to Theodosia,

"Well, it were one of them vet programmes. Ray comes in and says, would you fancy a biscuit with your tea? And all I could say was, *not now love, they are just giving a little monkey an enema.* They really had ought to warn you when they're going to show owt like that."

Monica had laughed inwardly all the way to the rehearsal room and couldn't resist reproducing the conversation for her colleagues, who found it hilarious. Now she was the one, sitting at home flicking through the channels, trying to avoid anything too graphic.

It wasn't very promising, just a rag tag collection of strange shouty programmes with toothless, tattooed people airing their problems on TV. Lots of things about antiques or cooking. No really good dramas to absorb her. She was half hoping to find her young self in a costume drama perhaps? Surely they were worth repeating? Her Lady Violette in Carwood House was worth reviving. It got fabulous reviews at the time, and her French accent was flawless, even Claudette had said so……But then, that was all so long ago, when she could learn her lines in a taxi on the way to the studio. Now she couldn't remember anything.

She remembered how she was often recognized by the public when she was playing Violette; those had been such wonderful days. Of course, "Theatre People" still knew her work and that's what really counted, the theatre. Television acting was an odd beast, strangely boring at best, utterly tedious at worst. She was happy where she was, treading the boards.

Something on the screen caught her eye, someone talking in a very rough and ready way, while a camera followed them about. They seemed to be knocking on people's doors. At first she couldn't understand what she was seeing. Was it some sort of documentary? No, it didn't seem to be, there was no commentary. And then she realized - this was the reality TV she had heard so much about. This was what was taking work from trained actors!

Monica spent the next an hour being appalled by what she saw. How could anyone watch this? This wasn't properly scripted, crafted entertainment, it was just…..well, rubbish. When it finally ended, she felt even more despondent. What was the world coming to? Thank God she had started out in the business all those years ago and not now.

It had grown quite dark by now. Even at four o'clock the evening had set in, making her feel even more isolated. This was the time of day when she would usually have been in her dressing room, starting to get ready for the show, feeling that buzz deep inside, that flutter of excitement. Silently she went around the room turning on the lamps before drawing the curtains. Normally Patty would be back by now to feed Theodosia, but tonight she would have to do it. Cat food and then her food. But then what, a long dark evening? She would be glad when it was bedtime. Tomorrow she would go out, be in the community. All this being on her own wasn't good for her. It would be better tomorrow. And as Claudette was so very fond of telling her, *there is always a way*.

Chapter Five

Monica's romantic ideas of wandering around the village would probably have worked well if it had been summer. She had imagined herself drifting around in a beautiful floral dress, with a huge straw hat on her head, feeling every inch the English lady. But in mid-winter, she felt as cold and brittle as the landscape. Huddled in her long overcoat she found herself frowning as she walked, as though the chill was a personal affront to her.

Her ideas of chatting to people came to nothing. Nobody wanted to stop to speak on such a cold day, and anyway she was virtually a stranger to most people. She was just "that actress woman", from The Stonehouse. She knew it was her own fault; she and Trevor should have made more of an effort to join in community events and mixed with the locals. When Claudette had moved in with them, she had made a point of meeting people, everyone knew her in the village. She had a knack of remembering the smallest detail about each person, she made them feel special and they loved her for it. But for Monica, all her neighbours seemed so very dull and parochial, compared with her acting friends. She had, on occasion, been approached to speak to the W.I. or similar groups, but frankly she would rather have taken sandpaper to her nipples than address a room full of mousey housewives in ugly sweaters and elasticated jeans.

She glanced forlornly in at Caraway's tea room, but inside she could just make out two old ladies with bowls in front of them. It looked like a sort of desperate soup kitchen rather than the buzzing hub of gossip she was hoping for. She felt a bit like a ghost, haunting the village unseen, whilst everyone else went about their useful lives. This wasn't how her break was meant to be, she was supposed to be relaxing.

Looking down the empty main street, Monica felt she had been chastised. The village had been there all this time. She had never bothered with it, and now that she needed it, it wasn't bothered about her. She turned up her collar and made her way home. The actress in her couldn't help but hope that she cut a dramatic lonely figure, striding home in her long black coat. Like the French Lieutenant's Woman, tragic but fascinating.

She let herself in by the back door, Patty would be there but she had no choice but to see her. Perhaps she could keep the conversation to a minimum? She wasn't in the mood to hear about having three piece suites recovered or whatever her cleaner's current tedious obsession was.

The first thing she saw as she stepped inside made her heart melt. Her beautiful Theodosia was sitting next to the range, her eyes squinting in ecstasy with the warmth. Then she heard Patty, talking in her never ending stream of truncated vowels, deftly wiping the surfaces as she went.

"Patty, hello," she said. "I've been for a walk. It's quite brisk out."

"That's one way o' puttin' it, I suppose. I was just saying to Theodosia, you can get stuck in a rut with your hair. Now me, I like to change mine every now and again. Shake things up a bit". She glanced at Monica's bob with obvious disapproval. "But other people keep the same style for years. Take my friend Vera, she's 'ad that same do for as long as I can remember. It's well overdue for a change. Last time she went to the hairdresser Hitler were just growing out his fringe."

Monica grimaced. "Well, there is something to be said for a classic cut, you know, Patty? When you get to our age, we should know what suits us." She knew Patty was a few years younger than her, but it was an eye for an eye in this sort of exchange.

Theodosia let out a long low purr of contentment. She was warm and had company, what else would she have wished for? Monica picked her up.

"You're a happy girl aren't you, sweetheart? Do you like having Mummy at home?" she said, kissing the cat on its head.

Patty frowned "Oh yes. I was meaning to ask, how long will you be *workin' from home*? Only I shall 'ave to know if I've to come back and feed her Ladyship." It was something Patty had done since Claudette had gone and now it had become so much a part of the routine that Monica hadn't given it a second thought. She knew there was no point continuing with the pretence so she said casually, "Oh, actually, I've decided to take a few days off. Trevor will be away, so Theodosia and I will have the place to ourselves. I thought it would be nice."

"You don't normally have a break durin' theatre season, do you?"

"No, I know, but last year was so tough, with mother and everything, I just felt I needed some time off."

"Mmm, I see. I do miss her, your mother. I miss my little chats with her, you know? She were always so interesting, always had something good to say. Anyway, what are you planning to do with this time off?"

All the time she was talking, Patty continued to tidy, clean and polish. She had spent a lifetime doing it, for her own family, and then other people's. Now it had become second nature. She knew exactly what needed to be done without a moment's thought, her large, capable hands skilfully creating order and cleanliness.

"Mmmmm, " said Monica, momentarily transfixed by Patty's nimble movements.

"Only, I wouldn't have thought that it was a right good time for an 'oliday. Most things'll be shut, won't they?"

"Well, I shan't be going far," said Monica snapping back into reality. "I thought I might spend some time here. Perhaps do a bit of gardening."

"Gardening? In't winter? Anyway, you have a gardener come."

"Well yes, but I'm not talking about the heavy stuff. Maybe I'll plant a few seeds, grow them indoors."

"Seeds!" said Patty as though she had never heard of such a thing. "Now, me, I don't like anything to do with seeds. It's all that germination, makes me go quite cold."

At times there really wasn't anything to say after one of Patty's bombshells and so, still holding Theodosia to her Monica said, "Anyway, I should get changed."

Sometimes, she reflected as she climbed the stairs, it was a good thing that Theodosia couldn't understand everything that was said to her. Listening to Patty droning on would have sent her insane. Instead she seemed to rather like the constant flow of conversation. God only knew why.

In the bedroom Monica took off her coat and hung it neatly away. Years of tiny dressing rooms had instilled in her a sense of carefulness where clothes were concerned. Everything back on the rack, everything in its place so you could find it during a quick change. It was who she was. But now she could throw everything in a heap, it wouldn't matter. She had all the time in the world, and she hated it.

She looked at the carefully made bed and for a moment considered another nap. The day stretched ahead, full of empty hours. Sleep would help it to pass. Suddenly snapping to, she felt angry with herself. In her mind she could hear her mother saying, *Sleeping away your day choupinette? Once it is gone, you will never get this day back. Tomorrow has not come, yesterday has gone, but now is what we have, so do not waste it.*

Monica brushed her hair in front of the mirror while Theodosia wandered amongst the cosmetics, gently patting one or two to the floor with her silvery velvet paw.

"Oh, darling don't do that! Don't knock Mummy's things on the floor. Naughty girl. What's this all about? Do you want attention, is that it? Well look, just let me finish with my hair and then you and I can have a lovely day together. We can….."

The cat looked at her with unblinking sapphire blue eyes.

"We can…." Monica realized she had no idea what she would do. Actresses worked. They weren't good at time off unless they went away somewhere. All her friends would be working, if they were lucky, and so it was up to her. What could she do? Usually when actors are "resting" they spend it fretting about and looking for the next job, but this was different. There was no "next job," she already had one, she just couldn't go back to it yet.

Damn Christian, damn her memory! Down below in the kitchen she could hear Patty singing one of her odd little songs, tuneless and meandering. Trevor called it, "Her bee in a jam jar impression" and for some reason today, it made Monica want to scream. And then plonk, plonk, plonk, one by one Theodosia was knocking the pots and palettes from her dressing table.

Overcome, she flopped down on the bed and stared into space. Why was it she was so good at being other people, but now she was alone and for once totally being herself, she just couldn't deal with it?

35

Chapter Six

When her tears had subsided, Monica felt relieved, purged even. She slowly picked up the things Theodosia had spattered about the bedroom floor and felt a strange sense of calm, nothing had really changed and yet she felt better.

After losing an acting role many years ago, a friend had said to her, "You'll feel better after you've had a good cry." She didn't and never had, not when she had failed at something, or when a show had closed early, not even when the family cats had died. Crying had never made her feel anything more than blotchy and exhausted. She wasn't a pretty crier, she knew that. She could fake it for a performance but in real life, she looked like a pig.

This time it had soothed her, like a balm to her ragged emotions. Something had been released and now she could go on again. It was just a few days off and nothing more. Just a few days of doing exactly as she damn well pleased. Instinctively she reached out for her cat, who had been watching her with round, alarmed eyes. Theodosia dodged out of her way, as though she didn't want to be infected by all this emotion. She flicked her tail and darted out of the room. Monica heard her footsteps on the stairs as she ran to safety.

After a few minutes Monica followed her downstairs. She could still hear Patty's unmusical singing coming from the lounge, so she went into

Trevor's book lined study. She stood in the doorway for a moment, taking in her husband's scent, a mixture of cigarettes, his face balm and Earl Grey tea. She missed him so much.

Then she closed her eyes, turned around twice with one finger outstretched, and decided that whichever book she was pointing at when she opened her eyes, was the one she would read from cover to cover, whatever it was. She didn't normally have the time or desire to read, especially if she was learning a script, so now would be the perfect time.

She opened one eye. She had it half in mind to cheat, particularly if she turned out to be pointing at one of Trevor's dull fishing books, but she was pleasantly surprised. *Rebecca*, by Daphne Du Maurier. She smiled. She had even been in a production of it a few years ago. She had played......oh, Max De Winter's sister, damn, what was her name? A no nonsense woman, always putting her foot in it..... No, the name had gone, it was just there on the edge of her memory and then it had slipped away completely.

She would try not to think about it, it would probably just pop into her head later. The thing was not to get obsessed with these things. She took the book into the lounge. She would sit in her favourite chair, curl up and disappear to Cornwall, and when it got dark, she would turn on a single lamp and read by it.

Theodosia greeted her cautiously, sniffing at her extended hand with suspicion. Having convinced herself that all was now well, she followed Monica to the armchair and jumped up beside, resting between the arm of the chair and Monica's thigh. Warm and relaxed she made the perfect companion.

Monica was one of those people who read every bit of a book. Any notes or prefaces at the start had to be looked at before she dived into the story, and she had barely read two pages when Patty came in.

"You're all right, I've done in here," she said. "Now then, would you mind if I get off a bit sharpish today, only it's me eldest's birthday and he's off into town with his mates. I want to make sure he eats summat before he goes."

Monica knew Patty's eldest son was at least thirty, and quite capable of looking after himself. But a mother was a mother, she supposed, and to be honest she was quite pleased at the thought of being left in peace, without the perpetual whine of Patty's tune free hum.

"No, no," she said, "by all means please do. I understand completely. I hope he has a lovely time."

"I doubt that very much," said Patty in a slightly lugubrious tone. "Well, you know, it'll be a usual lads' night out. Trev'll 'ave a korma and Kev'll 'ave a trauma and they'll all roll 'ome drunk as lords. That's the way it goes." Without waiting for a response she left the room.

Not for the first time Monica wondered what sort of mother she would have made. But her career had always driven her on and children really hadn't interested her until it was much too late. She had never been one to coo over babies and the whole giving birth thing seemed horrendous, but maybe, just maybe if she could suddenly have had some grown up children, she may have been a fabulous mummy. And then again maybe she wouldn't, she might have been an absolute nightmare. She would never have lived up to Claudette, that was for sure.

It had been natural for her mother, she loved to care for people and so it was inevitable that she would devote herself to her husband and her daughter. Not that Monica had been spoilt. Claudette was always strict and went to great lengths to make sure her daughter was the best person she could be, but never indulged or cosseted.

Claudette was Claudette, her own person, and she wanted that for Monique too. When she had first started going out with Trevor, her mother had said to her. *Whatever you do, Choupette keep hold of your career, one day it may be your saviour. Do not give up everything because you are in love. You cannot see it now, but life goes on after the wedding bells have stopped ringing.*

Smiling at the memory Monica went back to her book. Theodosia yawned and stretched out her front paw. Elongated and silvery it looked like moonlight. Monica smiled and carried on reading. Just as she had imagined, the light outside had gradually faded until they were left sitting a pool of light from the standard lamp. She and Theodosia together.

At around five, she rubbed her eyes and put the book down. She probably ought to wear her reading glasses, but it was such an admission of age, that she only put them on if she was really tired. Feeling stiff she struggled to her feet. Vivid images of the

Cornish coast and the aloof Max De Winter hovered in her mind. Languorously she stretched.

"Well, Theodosia, isn't it about time I got a pot of tea and some cake?"

So saying she made her way toward the kitchen. Just as she reached the doorway, a voice said, "Well, I'm not sure about tea and cake but if you throw in some smoked salmon, I may be interested."

It was a very clear voice, very cultured, with almost a sarcastic, superior edge to it."

Suddenly afraid, Monica turned around. Had someone got into the house while she was lost in her book? But the lounge was silent. Everything was in its place and Theodosia continued to look at her with a sphinx-like stare, giving no indication at all that she had heard anything amiss.

She stood there for a while keeping perfectly still, listening to every sound, but nothing happened, everything was normal. She went to the kitchen and clicked on the kettle. As she waited for it to boil a ridiculous thought came into her head. Smoked salmon? What if it was Theodosia speaking? Not out loud of course, but in her head, like ….Oh, what was the word? Come on brain…..Telepathy. No, no all actresses had over active imaginations, they couldn't act if they didn't. She was just being silly.

Even so, as she took her cake and tea back into the lounge she couldn't help but say out loud, "Did you really want some smoked salmon?"

Theodosia rolled over and waited for her stomach to be rubbed, but she *said* nothing.

Relaxing a little, Monica resumed her seat. There would be an explanation, there always was. The number of so called haunted theatres she had worked in over the years had done nothing to convince her of the existence of the supernatural. But what if they could communicate? What if she and Theodosia had such a special relationship, they could hear each other's thoughts. What if Claudette had something to do with it? No, no no, she had to stop this now. This was not healthy.

"Oh, that way madness lies!" she quoted and got to her feet. No, it was being cooped up at home, that was the problem. It just wasn't going to work, being at home doesn't suit her at all. She needed outside stimuli, she needed to work.

She decided she would ring Christian. There, his name was back and she was pretty sure she could remember her script now, after a break. She grabbed her mobile, pressed his number and waited. After a while Christian's voice came on the line. He was obviously talking to someone else as he answered. Distracted, he seemed a little surprised to hear her voice.

"Christian, hello! Thanks for the break, but I'm going crazy here. Can I come back tomorrow? You've been marvellous, you really have, but you can only work round me for so long and I need to be there."

"Monique? I was going to ring you later. How are you feeling?"

"Fine. Fighting fit, just bored to death. How is the production going?"

"Yeah, erm great, great. Thing is, sweetheart, we've had to carry on. Sam has been standing in for you and……we've sort of decided to go with her. We didn't know if you were coming back, it isn't personal or anything."

"Sam? Sam is in her twenties! How is she going to play a middle aged mother?"

We're working on her makeup, she'll be fine. She really is doing a good job. I can't just take the part away from her."

"No, but you're happy to take it away from me. Well, thank you, Christian, thank you very much."

Viciously Monica jabbed the "End Call" button. Shaking with a mixture of anger and grief she felt a sob begin to rise. Theodosia looked up at the sound. It confused her and so she closed her eyes, wrapped her tail over her nose and pretended to go to sleep. She didn't like too much emotion.

Not knowing what to do, Monica wandered about the room. The enormity of the conversation was still sinking in. SHE HAD BEEN SACKED! What would she do? She had never been sacked in the entirety of her thirty year career. Sacked by snivelling little Christian. How dare he? It really was the end when young women were taking older actresses' parts. Didn't they have enough of their own? Her rage grew steadily.

So, this is where she was in her life: on the scrap heap, no job, and no real friends to speak of. Her fabulous career had given her nothing, absolutely nothing. God, it was a mess. What was she going to do? She needed to speak to Trevor, but he would be preparing for the evening performance.

The feelings from that terrible day when she had been sent home started to resurface. Was this really it? The end of the road? How long before word got around that she had been let go? That she wasn't up to it any more? No more acting. All that experience going to waste. What would she do?

Almost without thinking she went to the drinks cupboard and pulled out the second best whisky.

Chapter Seven

When Monica finally woke from her oblivion, she found she could not remember getting to bed. She had vague memories of watching something on T.V. although she couldn't remember what it was, and then nothing. A huge blank. Her head ached right from the bridge of her nose up into her skull. Cautiously she pulled herself up on her pillows.

From under the duvet marched a somewhat indignant Theodosia, who no doubt had enjoyed a good night's sleep on her comatose owner. She stalked up the bed on stiff legs and meowed into Monica's face. A waft of fishy breath floated over her dainty fangs and made Monica's stomach churn.

"Hello, Theodosia," Monica said, turning her face away. "I'll get up in a moment, just give Mummy a minute." She grabbed the little carriage clock from her bedside table and looked at the time. It was 10.30. Worse than she thought, she had slept the morning away. Instinctively she pulled back the covers and tried to quickly get to her feet. As she did so she found that she felt oddly light and "swirly," as though last night's Scotch hadn't worn off.

She wiped a hand over her clammy neck and realised just how stupid she'd been. Now, as well as all her other problems, she had a hangover. Suddenly she felt hot and then nauseous.

After being sick Monica felt initially a little better, but her head ached like someone had dried her brain out and was now squeezing it at regular intervals. She made herself go downstairs, carefully avoiding Theodosia who was determined to run back and forth under her feet all the way to the bottom of the steps.

Slowly she made her way to the kitchen and weakly poured herself a glass of water. She felt so dry and old, at this point she couldn't imagine ever feeling well again. She hated what she had done to herself. Touching her face she realized she still had her make up on and her face felt stiff and dirty. What a state to be in.

Theodosia had started her incessant breakfast call, weaving back and forth at Monica's feet, occasionally hopping up and tapping her on the leg.

"Wer-ow, wer-ow, wer-ow, wer-ow, wer-ow!" Theodosia's tone became more and more strident. Breakfast was late. Reluctantly Monica bent to the cupboard under the sink. There was the cat food........*Juicy chunks in a tasty jelly*. She felt herself begin to heave and grabbed the pack of kibble next to it.

Opening it at arm's length, she quickly tipped some of the biscuits into a bowl and placed them on the floor. Theodosia looked at the contents of the bowl and then at Monica. Cats don't have many facial expressions, but as anyone who has ever lived with one will confirm, they have just as many as they need. The look of utter disdain on Theodosia's pretty silvery face could not be misunderstood in any way. This was not acceptable! This was not the breakfast she wanted!

Stooping to sniff the bowl for a second, the cat's disappointment was obvious. She gave a little dainty wretch, scraped the floor around the bowl comprehensively and then walked away, flicking her tail. Hard tack is not what is required at breakfast time.

As much as she loved her cat, Monica could not have dealt with squidgy lumps of cat food that morning. Forlornly she sat down at the kitchen table. The paracetamol pills were in the bathroom cabinet, but they were ALL THE WAY upstairs. She sat sipping her water, staring into space. All she could think of was how ill she felt. She hadn't been drunk in years. This was such a horrible mistake, but once you've done it there can be no going back, and so she was resigned to her punishment. Full of queasy self-pity, she let out a long, suffering sigh.

Her suffering was about to increase tenfold as Patty came in from the garden. Taking care that the cat wasn't near the back door she quickly slipped in.

"Just been to the bins!" she announced. "All right, are you? You look terrible."

"I'm fine, Patty. I just had a late night."

Monica cringed inwardly. It had seemed such a wonderful luxury to have a cleaner when she was out working, but now it just felt like an intrusion. She would have given anything to spend the morning alone whilst she gradually got to grips with things, If she could get to grips with things? She wasn't at all sure that she could. From where she was at that precise moment she felt like a survivor sitting in the wreckage of her life.

"'Nother nippy one," remarked Patty, washing her hands at the sink. I'm going over to my niece's later on. I shall have to wrap up, it's right out in the middle of nowhere. Barn conversion, it is."

Monica's head pounded and just wanted Patty to be quiet.

Patty went on, "They tell me they are The Thing now, barn conversions, but I wouldn't want one. Something second hand from cows? No, it's not for me. She's done it up nice, I'll give her that, she's got some lovely things. Last time I went she were showing me what she'd bought - two wooden seagulls in a box. Daft looking thing it were but, do you know, in her house it looked perfect? Funny that, must be something to do with it being a barn, I suppose."

Monica knew the talking wouldn't stop. So long as Patty had an audience she would go on and so, dragging herself to her feet, she said,

"Patty, you know, you're right. I don't feel too good, I think I'll go back to bed for a while."

"Just as you like, Mrs P. I've got a fair bit to do. I won't shout when I go, just in case you're asleep."

"That's very kind," said Monica and made her way slowly towards the stairs. Theodosia, who was still sulking about her food, watched her pass along the hall, not sure whether to follow her, or continue to make her point about biscuits at breakfast time. In the end she decided to stay put, she was comfortable.

As Monica reached the first landing, Patty called after her. "You go on up and rest. Like I said to our Paul when he got in last night.... best to sleep it off."

Monica didn't reply. Patty clearly knew what had been going on and somehow that made it a million times worse. She lay down on the bed and closed her eyes. Unsettled for a moment, it felt like the bed was slowly rotating. Opening one eye, she watched the mirrored wardrobe door move across her line of vision. This was too grim, she couldn't even close her eyes and escape from herself.

Nauseous again, she stood up and went to the bathroom. Hot and uncomfortable, she reached for the paracetamol and swallowed two straight down without even stopping for water. Something had to make her feel better. As she closed the bathroom cabinet door she caught sight of herself. Patchy make up on a puffy, grey face. She turned away and retreated back to bed.

Not knowing what else to do she lay down and clung on to the bed, hoping that it would eventually stop turning.

When she woke again, her head had stopped aching. Her mouth felt dry and sour, but the room had finished rotating and she did at least feel a little bit more human.

She didn't get up, feeling content just to lie there in relative comfort for a while. Without knowing it Monica almost immediately drifted off into a peaceful sleep, the sort that you have when your pain has stopped or your worries are suddenly resolved. When she came to again, she felt cool and rested. It was hard to believe she had thought she was dying a few hours before.

After a hot shower and warm towels straight from the heated rail, she began to feel a little bit more normal. Her stomach still felt weak and the odd ache here and there made her feel as though she had been beaten up, but on the whole she was better. This had been a horrible mistake and one that would not be repeated.

When she was finally up she decided on a cup of good strong coffee, but as the machine did its work, the smell began to make her feel ill again and so she sat miserably at the kitchen table with a very feeble cup of instant. Until that moment, she had been concentrating on her physical discomfort, but now her mind turned back to the root of her problem. She had been sacked.

She still couldn't make the word mean anything, it wouldn't go in. She had never been replaced, ever. Why hadn't Christian had the decency to call her and talk about it? Why just get someone else? So, she had forgotten her lines a couple of times; everyone dries now and then, for God's sake. He should have been pleased to be working with an experienced actress, instead of these half trained regional people they turned out from drama school these days. Most of them couldn't do decent RP if their lives depended on it.   And Sam! What was Sam? A bit of a girl. She was always trailing off at the end of lines, nobody past the first two rows would have a clue what she was mumbling about!

How dare he sack her! He was a little nobody, a nothing! A skinny little runt with a high opinion of himself.

Monica continued to rage into her coffee. What she needed was to speak to Trevor. She checked her watch, it was worth a try. She got her phone and dialled.

"Mon? How's rehearsal going?" Trevor's voice was so perfect, she had fallen in love with it, even before she had loved the man. Rich and clear, she never failed to get a little thrill whenever she heard it. Today she needed him more than ever.

"Mon? Are you okay?"

There was no good way to tell him, so after a pause she said, calmly, "Trevor, I've been sacked." There was a silence at the end of the line. "Trevor? Darling? Did you hear what I said?" For a second all she could hear was a jumble of voices and noises and then at last her husband's voice.

"What? Who the hell would sack **you**?"

"Christian bloody Groves, that's who. Little shit."

"But why? Did you have a row? What happened?"

"No, it's this memory thing. I forgot my lines a couple of times, so he sent me home, all sweetness and light, 'Have a rest, Monique, don't worry, Monique,' and then when I wanted to go back, he'd given my part away."

"To whom, darling?"

"Oh, Sam. You wouldn't know her. She's a nothing, only about fifteen and she'll be playing a middle aged mother. Well, good luck with that!"

"It'll be a disaster."

"I know, but it's not my problem now, is it? I'm no longer required."

Just talking to Trevor was helping. She could almost feel the fire coming back into her belly. It had always been the two of them against the world and this would be no different.

"They will pay you though, won't they, for what you've done? Have you spoken to Clara?"

"Not yet, not yet. I've just been in shock. This problem with my memory is beginning to worry me. You don't think I've got Alzheimer's, do you?"

"No, of course not. You're just tired. You've had a lot to deal with since, well, since your mother..."

"Maybe I should take some time off?"

"Good idea, have a few days to think. Look, darling, I'll have to go in a minute."

"Yes, I know. Don't you get sacked too. God, sacked! It's an awful bloody word. You know what, Trevor? I'm not going to be sacked ever again."

"Mon?"

"No, because I've decided to retire. Things are changing out there, we aren't valued. I'm a bloody good actress and if they don't appreciate me, they don't deserve me!"

"Now, don't be silly, Monica, you can't retire. We'll both go on 'till we drop, you know that. They'll have to carry us out."

"No, I mean it. It's time this old bird got out of the business, time I had a bit of a life."

"And do what?" said Trevor, with a slightly teasing edge to his voice.

"Hundreds of things. All those things I've never had time for: reading, learning the piano, dance classes, art, hundreds of things."

"Flower arranging? Embroidery? Okay, okay, I'll give you six months and then you'll be going crazy. Look, I really have to go. Call Clara, ask her about the money and tell her you're retiring. See what she says! I love you darling. Look I'll try and get home if I can. Bye - bye."

The phone went dead. But instead of feeling deserted Monica felt liberated. She really would retire! Nobody would treat her like that again. She had had a wonderful career and now it was time to do other things.

She put the phone down on the worktop and wandered into the living room. She would start looking for classes today.

"It's a good idea, isn't it, Theodosia? You'd like me to be at home more, wouldn't you?"

The cat didn't respond. She was in a tightly curled ball, snoring rhythmically. Smiling to herself, Monica remembered "the voice" she thought she'd heard last night. She really was tired. But, she had to admit that if Theodosia could speak, she would have a voice just like the one her mind had created for her.

Chapter Eight

Clara's voice was as dynamic as ever. She had been Monica and Trevor's agent for sixteen years but her passion had never dimmed. She always seemed delighted to hear from her clients, whether they were just starting out or seasoned performers who had been on her books for years.

Monica knew it must have been faked, but she was so good at it, it was hard to mind. Enthusiasm was her business. Somehow she managed to speak to each person as though she loved everything about them and remembered every role they'd ever been cast in.

"Monique! My favourite Hamlet's mummy. How are you? Don't tell me your run is coming to an end already?"

For once Monica wished that Clara wasn't quite so full of gusto. She had played Gertrude four years ago, and now, in her overwrought, sensitive state she wondered if that meant she had been lousy in everything else since. Taking a breath she said, "Clara, I've had to leave *Like Lemon Drops*."

"But why? Are you ill? I thought you loved the role."

"Yes, I did, but I was told to take a break and then told not to come back."

"By Christian Groves? He's usually an angel to work with. Did you argue? What happened?"

"No, nothing like that. I just forgot my lines a few times and he's obviously got a problem with older women, that's all. Maybe he feels threatened, I don't know. Anyway, I'm at home. Can you give him a call and make sure I get paid for the rehearsal time, at least? I might as well get something out of the snidey little sod."

"Yes, yes I will. Do you know if he's looking for a replacement?"

"He's got one, she's about twelve. Ask him yourself."

Slightly annoyed by Clara's immediate concern to find a substitute, Monica began to feel just a little bit excited by the shock she was about to deliver.

"Right, right, well I'll ring him this afternoon and sort it out. In the meantime we need to get you working. Do you fancy *Top Girls*? They're reviving it at the Almeida, could transfer to the West End. Pope Joan might suit you? Interested?"

"No, I don't think so," answered Monica, delaying the moment when she would make her announcement.

"Are you sure? It's a good time to be doing it, what with the recession, still relevant……. Well, okay let me see who else is casting."

"No, actually, Clara I've decided to retire." It had the desired effect. Clara went silent. "I've had enough," Monica went on. "I've enjoyed myself, but now it's time to leave the party and let the young ones carry on."

"You can't retire, Monique! Don't be silly. This is all bloody Christian's fault. Let me call him…."

"It isn't his fault. I just think it's time to stop. It isn't the same business as when I started out."

"Monique, look, don't say that's it. Maybe we could just tone it down. Work when you like, pick and choose a little."

"No, that would never happen. I'd always say yes to work, you know I would, and then I'd be back to square one. I want to spend more time at home. I have a lovely house in a lovely location and I've hardly spent any time here."

"What does Trevor think?"

"He laughed at me, but I mean it. No more shabby dressing rooms, no more late nights, no more evil critics…."

"Okay, okay so the theatre is gone. How about voice over work?"

Monica said nothing.

"You wouldn't have to worry about makeup, or costumes. You just go in, do your bit and collect the fee. A lot of my clients love an ad campaign. And forgetting lines? No problem, they'll be there in front of you."

Clara obviously thought she had found the perfect solution; she kept her client and her client kept her income.

The ominous silence at the end of the line prevailed.

"Monique?"

"Well, thank you very much," began Monica, stonily. "You have just confirmed my opinion of the so called acting profession as it is today. Voice over work, Clara? I did not train at RADA and then spend years perfecting my craft to be the voice of a talking tampon!"

Monica ended the call abruptly. Theodosia looked up questioningly from her bird watching spot on the window ledge.

Was she really that washed up, that her own agent was suggesting voice overs? Despondently she put down the phone and paced around the lounge. She really needed to get on with her life. Her new life, here in the village. She needed to put all this behind her and forge new friendships.

She picked up the notes she had made about possible local activities. At the top of the list was, "Book Club, library 10.30 Friday." Today was Friday. Why not take the bull by the horns, go along and join? She moved towards the door. She would need to change, but what did one wear for a book club? Maybe she should look like an author, a little eccentric and arty….. then maybe she wasn't quite prepared for this, perhaps next week would be better when she had had time to think about it?

A clattering noise in the hall and Theodosia's wide eyed interest heralded Patty's arrival. Quickly putting her notes aside, Monica went out to meet her. Sooner or later she would have to tell Patty that she was no longer required. After all, if she was to be at home, she wouldn't need a cleaner.

"Morning, Mrs P. I thought I'd start with her ladyship's litter tray this morning. It needs a proper good clean out." Monica decided not to do anything hasty. Patty had been with them such a long time, it would seem strange not to have her around any more, annoying though she was.

In a fit of guilt and maybe just a little desperation, Monica said, "No, come and have a cup of tea with me in the kitchen before you start. It's so cold this morning, come and warm up."

Seemingly unimpressed, Patty sauntered into the other room with Theodosia following closely, rubbing her lilac face fervently on Patty's shopping bag, by way of a greeting.

"Shall I make it then?" asked Patty, as Monica took a seat at the table.

"Oh, er, yes…. Thank you."

Theodosia hopped lightly up onto Monica's lap, and made it quite clear that she was preparing to be entertained by the humans. Monica had often wondered how her cat managed to convey exactly how she felt without a single word. What an actress she would have made.

Whilst Patty went about boiling the kettle and preparing the tea, Monica sat awkwardly waiting. She was half regretting this invitation to "chat" but now she had to get on with it.

Patty brought two mugs over and sat down heavily at the table.

"Nice to take the weight off," she commented. "Been up since five, doing the ironing. Stephen's going away for the weekend with his young lady."

Stephen was Patty's middle son, a plump Billy Bunterish lad who occasionally picked his mother up from work.

"That's nice. Where are they going?" ventured Monica.

"Oh, don't ask me, Penrith or Penzance. Somewhere like that anyway...."

"And what about you, Patty? Are you doing anything nice over the weekend?" The conversation was just as awkward as Monica feared but she was determined to persist. After all, she would need to speak to all kinds of people in her new life.

"To tell you the truth," answered Patty, "I've been invited to a party."

"How lovely. What sort of party?"

"Well, it's back up in Yorkshire. It's me cousin, Ken. He'll be 80 this coming week."

"That's a marvellous age to reach. I hope you have a good time."

"I might not go yet."

"Oh you must. It'll be nice to go back home and see everyone. These things don't happen often."

"I know, but it's a long way and to be honest I've never been that keen on Ken. He's a bit odd."

Despite herself Monica had to ask. She had to know what constituted odd in her cleaner's eyes. "In what way, odd?"

"Well, he were a sickly child. We all used to call him Kidney Ken, in the family. Always off sick from school, never playing out or anything. Anyway, his mother, me Anty Elsie, doted on him."

"That's only natural I suppose, if he was poorly."

"Aye, I know but I think it sent him a bit strange. When he were about seven or eight he saw a film at The Regent in Thirsk. *Blood and Sand* with Tyrone Power. Do you know it?"

Monica shook her head, wondering what strange and wonderful path Patty was taking her down. Theodosia gave a little huff, which for just an instant sounded like a smothered laugh.

"It were about bull fighting, and Ken's mother did no more than make him the complete matador's outfit, and in them days materials were difficult to come by. Anyway, she managed it somehow. He wore it for years, they couldn't get him out of it. Before my time, but I've seen the photos."

"Oh Patty, that doesn't sound so bad. I loved dressing up. He was a little boy. Being ill all the time probably made him imaginative, that's all."

"Well, if you say so, but then there were all the business with Petula Clark."

Monica felt a very strong urge to change the subject, but there it was dangling in the air......*The business with Petula Clark*. Could she really leave it alone? Hating herself just a little, Monica said, "Petula Clark?"

"Oh, mad on her, he were. Collected all her records, saw all her films. Then he started going to the concerts. All the way to London he'd go, on his own. Anywhere she was on, he'd go."

"Well that's all right, isn't it? He was a fan"

"Yes, it would have been but it got out of hand. He was what you'd call a stalker nowadays. Like I said, he's a bit of an odd one is Ken."

There was something about talking to Patty that always made Monica feeling slightly depressed, as though there was a darkness in her that seeped out and clouded everything. She had to avoid these chats, they were no good for her. Picking up her tea and placing Theodosia under her arm she said, "Well, I'll let you get on. I thought I might go to the Book Club this morning. So, I'll need to pop up and get changed."

Chapter Nine

Monica eventually decided on a dark blue cable knit sweater, jeans and a large white fringed scarf. She looked at her reflection in the wardrobe door and decided that she had it just about right. Arty, but not too pretentious.

Of course she wouldn't know what they had been reading, but as an actress it wasn't as though she was unfamiliar with literature. She was sure to be able to discuss Dickens, Waugh and T.S. Eliot quite easily and they were bound to be kindred spirits, after all she wasn't going to a Bingo club. They would all have something in common, a love of the written word.

She took one last look at herself, smiled and went downstairs to announce her departure. Book Club, whatever it was like, had to be better than conversing with Patty about her strange family.

"I'm just off, Patty. It's only for an hour and a half, so I'll see you later."

Patty looked up from mopping the hall floor.

"Mind you don't slip," she said, and returned to her work.

The Book Club was in the village library, an unprepossessing 1960's single-story building, with ranch style white fencing and a hurriedly built disabled access ramp at the front. Without hesitation she went through the smoked glass automatic doors and approached the counter. She hadn't been in a library for years but despite modern technology they still looked and smelled exactly the same, like a school without the disinfectant.

The untidy, plump woman on the main reception desk looked up from her computer as Monica arrived. "Silver Surfer's Safe Shopping Slot has been cancelled," she said. "Didn't you get the email? Sorry."

"Sorry, the what?" said Monica. "I'm here for Book Club."

"Oh, sorry. One of our silver surfers looks just like you, must be your hair," said the woman, cheerily. "Now, are you a member of the club already? Cos there's a form to fill out, if not."

"Well, I'm a little late, so couldn't I do it afterwards?"

"Won't take long, I'll just photocopy a form for you. Hold on, I'll see if Sheila has got it."

And with that she waddled out from behind her desk and disappeared in search of the one and only form they appeared to have. Monica was very tempted to try and find the club on her own, after all it was only a little library. But manners got the better of her and so she stood and waited.

In the main body of the building a group of very small children were singing an unintelligible song, which seemed to involve a lot of clapping and wagging of elbows. Now, that was new, singing in a library. What happened to the hushes and stern looks from crusty librarians?

At length the receptionist returned with the form. "I'll just get this copied for you then," she said.

It was infuriating. Not for one minute had Monica envisaged such a fuss. Surely one just went in and discussed books; why did there have to be a form?

The form was duly copied and presented to her. A piece of A4 paper with "Do Not Remove" scrawled in the top right hand corner. Monica filled it out reluctantly, sighing as she did so. As far as she could tell there was nothing on it that had anything to do with her suitability to join the club, but she suffered it. By now she was ten minutes late. She hated being late, it was the ultimate in discourtesy.

Finally handing over the form she said, "So, where is the club taking place?"

"Just in the side room, there. They've only just started. Oh, by the way, are you a member of the library?"

"Well, no actually I'm not."

"Oh, right, well I'll get you an application form. Have you got three forms of identification with you?"

"Look, I really want to go and get started. Have the form ready for me and I'll collect it on the way out." Without waiting for a reply Monica walked quickly over, knocked on the glass panel of the door and went in. If she filled any more forms in the club would be over.

As Monica entered the featureless beige carpeted room, six surprised faces turned towards her. They obviously weren't used to new members.

A young woman of around twenty, with long straight hair and a tight smile, said, "Can I help you?"

"I'm here for the Book Club. I'm Monica."

"I see. Well, you'd better take a seat. I'm Tamsin, I run the group."

This wasn't the warm welcome from like-minded people she had expected. Looking around she saw a pile of plastic chairs leaning against the radiator. Grabbing the top one and noisily untangling it, she was aware that all eyes were on her. Gratefully she sat down. She smiled and said, "So, what are all your names?"

"We'll do the introductions later, Monica. We were just about to get some comments on *Indelible Link* by Susannah Straun."

Feeling chastened, Monica sank back into her seat a little. *Oh well, early days,* she thought.

"So, Jill, let's go to you first. What did you think?"

Jill was a grey looking little woman, who held her hands earnestly together as though constantly in prayer. She spoke in a quiet tone with a strong Oxfordshire bur. "Well, I thought it was very good. I mean when you find out that little tot has such a terrible disease, it's heartbreaking, and then when her mother abandons her, well."

"What sort of mother is that? I thought she was a horrible woman," chipped in a large lady brandishing the book as she spoke. "I don't know about wanting to find her. I'd have wanted nothing to do with her."

"But," said Tamsin sharply, "isn't the whole point that she needs to find her to achieve some sort of closure?"

"Have you read the book?" said the large lady, turning to Monica.

"No, I'm afraid not."

"Well, it's about this awful woman who has a very poorly kiddie and then dumps her in a bus station in Arbroath…."

"Oh," said Monica, she didn't know what else to say. It sounded extremely depressing and not the sort of thing she would want to read.

"It's based on a true story," added Tamsin, sternly.

The discussion continued in this vein for some time and it seemed to Monica that it was about whether or not the woman deserved to be a mother, rather than the book itself.

"Was it well written?" she ventured.

The ladies looked at her and for a moment said nothing. Then Jill said meekly, "Well, I enjoyed it." At this point, Monica had accidently ended the discussion.

"Shall we have our coffee now? And then we'll talk about next month's book, *Sofia and Son* by Ingrid Lowstein" said Tamsin, shooting her a glance and adding, "Coffee is ten pence, Monica. Just put the money in the jar."

All Monica had with her were her keys and so she had to hang around uncomfortably as they others helped themselves. She tried to start conversations with a couple of the women, but most of them seemed to know each other and each other's families, and she could hear various children's names being mentioned. At last Jill crept a little closer to her and enquired, "Do you have grandchildren, Monica?"

"Er no, I don't have any children actually. I'm an actress by trade you see. That takes up most of your time."

In the past when she had found herself in these situations, mentioning that she acted had always elicited a stir of excitement. But in this case it was met with an simple, "Oh"

Tamsin made her way over and said coolly, "You can borrow *Indelible Link*, at the front desk if you wish, and get a copy of our reading list at the same time."

By now Monica was wondering if she really wanted to see the reading list. "Did I hear you say you are an actress?" added Tamsin, unexpectedly.

"Yes, that's right."

"Oh, would we know you?"

"Well, I do mainly stage work, but you might remember me from Carwood House. I was Lady Violette?"

Tamsin shook her head. "And you aren't married I gather?"

"No, whatever gave you that idea? I've been married for twenty-seven years."

"Oh, it's just you said you had no children, so I assumed... Anyway, why Book Club, aren't you acting at present?"

The question ricocheted around her head for a moment. *Aren't you acting at present?* It was a hard question to answer, so she said, "No, not just at the moment."

"Resting, they say, don't they?" added Tamsin, with a slight hint of condescension in her voice. "Well, we'd better get back to the discussion."

As Monica glumly resumed her seat, already she sensed that this was not going to be the answer to her new life. If anything it had only served to highlight just how little she had in common with people outside the rarefied atmosphere of the theatre.

"Now, this next book," Tamsin said when they had all settled down, "has many similarities with the one we read two months ago. It isn't based on a true story, but it is researched from actual cases, so I think you're going to enjoy it."

She held up the book on the cover of which was an anguished looking woman holding her head in her hands.

"Has anyone read any Ingrid Lowstein before?"

Jill held up a timorous finger. "I have, the one about the little girl who was dying."

"Oh yes, *This Time Next Year*. So sad," said the big woman. "I've read that too."

"Well," said Tamsin, "this is about Sofia, who discovers that her only son has Autism and ADHD, and it's about her journey and how she comes to terms with it."

Monica sat through the rest of the session saying as little as possible. She knew she wouldn't be filling in the form that was waiting for her at reception. It might make things difficult if she bumped into any of them in the village, but she had made up her mind. She didn't want to come again to this closed little shop of mothers with their deadly books about dying children.

As the others were all saying goodbye at the end of the session, Monica slipped away unnoticed. Nobody bothered to say, "See you next time." Not even the receptionist enquired if she still wanted to join the library. It must have been very clear to them that she was a square peg in a round hole.

Monica walked back through the frosty streets of the village. Here and there the sun had started to touch the Cotswold stone of the buildings, leaving them dark and wet, but even the hint of spring sunshine didn't raise her spirits.

The odd thing she thought, was that when she had talked about her acting it was in the present tense. Was she really ready to retire? What else would there be to say about herself if not that?

At the Stonehouse, Patty was preparing to leave. As Monica came in through the back door, she was just pulling her coat on.

"Oh, 'ello. How was your club?" she said.

"To be honest, Patty it wasn't really my cup of tea."

"No, well, I didn't like to say. I didn't think it were. What you need is summat where you can perform. What about a choir, it'd take your mind off things? Like them women on the telly that sang so they wouldn't keep thinking about their husbands getting blown up in Afghanistan. Did 'em the world of good, it did. Some of 'em quite blossomed."

"Mmm," said Monica, doubtfully. A choir didn't seem much fun to her. Why would you want to be with everyone else and not out at the front by yourself? "So, Patty, have you decided, are you going to Kidney Ken's party?"

"No, I don't think so. I don't fancy it, and to be honest I don't think I've got anything suitable to wear around an unmarried man in his eighties."

Before Monica was forced to think of a suitable comment, Theodosia arrived and started batting the bottom of her enticingly fringed scarf.

Chapter Ten

Looking down at the cat happily chewing Monica's scarf, Patty huffed. "Look at you? You're as soft as butter with that cat, always were. I don't know why you don't get another one. It'd would do you good, both of you! Liven the place up a bit. Her Ladyship isn't getting any younger you know? I've noticed she spends a lot more time sleeping than she used to."

"Oh, no, Patty. We're fine as we are, aren't we, Theodosia? You don't want a friend, do you?"

The cat paused for a moment from her game and let out a plaintive meow. "There you are, Patty. She said no!"

"Well, I still think it would be a good idea. What you want to get is an active little kitten. It'd brighten you up no end. You'd be a different person, out and about in no time with one of them running around. My Antie Jean got a cockatiel after Uncle Frank died and it really brought her out of herself. She called him Savalas, after Kojak."

Theodosia suddenly stopped the game and stalked over to her litter tray in the corner. She had obviously heard enough. Flicking her tail she disappeared inside.

"Anyway, I must be off. But think on, it'd take your mind off things."

Once again Monica was left with the uncomfortable feeling that Patty knew more about what was going on in her life than she would have liked. But as she watched her cleaner trudge stoically down the path she realized, that in an odd way, if she did stop Patty coming, she would actually quite miss her.

She sat down at the kitchen table and wondered what to do with her day. Book Club had been an unmitigated disaster and she wasn't ready to try anything else on her list just yet. She made herself a coffee. It was what Trevor would have called a 'recreational' coffee, i.e. she didn't really want it, it was just something to do.

As she sat pondering, a photograph on the fridge caught Monica's eye. Along with the many cast photos and end-of-run party shots was a picture of a very young Theodosia. So tiny that she was dwarfed by the scatter cushion that sat next to her. With huge bat ears, her open, confident little face shone out. The lines of her face were still soft, yet to form the angular Siamese face she had now, and she was looking straight at the camera with an eagerness about her that had long gone.

A little wave of sadness came over Monica, as she realized Patty was right. Time had meanly run on, and Theodosia was ageing. She remembered only too well the day she had first brought her kitten home. Her friend Clive had surprised her with the cat at the end of a particularly long run at the RSC. It had been the most wonderful gift. Although she had grown up with her mother's Siamese she had never actually owned one herself. She had felt like a child watching the tiny silvery face poke out from the box Clive was using to conceal her. This kitten was not waiting for her cue, she pushed her head out and wailed in such an indignant way that Clive couldn't make his planned little speech. Madame Theodosia had stolen the scene.

And that was Theodosia, not a shy, timid little kitten, but a fully grown cat in a kitten's body. She was totally fearless. She complained bitterly on the drive back from Stratford. Clearly a cardboard box was not how she expected to be transported. Once inside the house, she took on the air of a prospective lodger, deciding if the digs would do or not.

She sniffed at corners, inspected the kitchen, ventured out into the hall to look at the stairs. It seemed to meet with her approval and so she decided to stay. But make no mistake, Theodosia had decided she was in charge from day one.

She spent the first few weeks being addressed as Theda, but when it became apparent that people were mishearing it as Freda, it was changed to the altogether grander Theodosia. Not that it really mattered since she ignored both names. At one stage Monica had taken to creeping up behind her and clapping her hands sharply, just to make sure that there was nothing wrong with her hearing.

The first unexpected side of Theodosia's nature was her destructiveness. All Claudette's kittens had scratched and chewed the odd thing but Theodosia was like a one cat demolition team. It wasn't so much that she was clumsy it was just that she seemed to have a total disregard for other people's property. If it was in the way, she moved it. If it needed to be altered, she applied her claws.

At first, Monica dreaded returning home each night, dreading what she was going to find. Both Trevor and she had work and apart from Patty's visits, for the most part Theodosia was alone. Later on when Claudette had come to live with them it hadn't been an issue, but for those first few months Monica wondered if perhaps she had done the wrong thing.

Claudette was appalled. "How can you have such a bright little girl and leave her alone like that? The devil, he will make work for idle paws." she scolded. "One day you will return and she will have gone to live with her Grand-mere."

"Mother, that's all well and good but I've never had a kitten before. She plays havoc with everything in the house. Why couldn't I have got one like Jason on Blue Peter? He just sat there, he was never naughty."

Claudette shrugged. "Jason? Hmm. He, Choupette, was drugged."

"Mother! He wasn't. It was a children's programme, they never would have allowed such a thing."

"Okay, think what you like, but have you ever seen a Siamese behave like that? No, and you will not. Drugged, drugged, drugged. It was the 60's"

"Mother, can we stick to Theodosia. She's driving me quite insane! Yesterday I opened one of the kitchen cupboards and she sprang out at me. I nearly had a heart attack, she's making me a nervous wreck."

"Monique," said Claudette, holding up her hand in censure. "Listen to me. First, I have told you many times, if you have two cats it will always be better, but you will not, so you have to be mother, playmate and friend all at once. And two, and most importantly, a Siamese will love you with all its heart and if you cannot love them back in the same way, then a Siamese is not for you. You have to love the chaos they bring, you have to love them."

But Monica found it difficult to love the chaos. It had been a long time since her mother had had a kitten. She had forgotten just how wild they could be, how they would tear around a room without touching the floor and then suddenly fall asleep as though their batteries had run low. Her mother's old cats would sleep, eat and potter about, they knew they weren't allowed to touch certain things or walk on certain surfaces, and so they didn't.

But Theodosia, oh Theodosia! She was a different matter. One morning, just as Monica was about to leave for the theatre, she went to make sure the kitten was safe. After searching every room she started to panic. Could she have slipped out? Climbed out of a window? Found a secret hiding place? Beginning to feel slightly fearful Monica called out, "Theodosia! Theodosia! Darling, come to Mummy!" It was met with silence. She tried again, this time walking through each room slowly, all the time calling to the cat whilst peering under furniture and opening cupboards.

The ground floor seemed to be empty so she climbed the stairs, still calling. From the landing she could see that her bedroom door was slightly ajar. She **had** to be in there. She wasn't allowed in normally but she must have somehow squeezed in through the gap.

Monica opened the door and walked in, fully expecting to see the kitten curled up on the duvet. But the room was empty. Under the bed! She must be under the bed. Getting down on all fours and starting to feel slightly irritated, Monica peered into the darkness. Nothing!

Having checked the wardrobe, the linen basket and even several drawers there was no sign. In exasperation she called out, "Theodosia! Come on now. Mummy has to go to work." Still nothing, but as she turned to leave the room she heard the tiniest squeak.

"Theodosia?" she called. Again a tiny muffled meow. "Darling, where are you?" she said, slowly moving around the room desperately trying to hear where the noise was coming from. "Sweetheart, talk to Mummy!" There it was again. This time, it was clearly coming from under the bed.

Scrambling down onto her knees again, Monica was hoping to see Theodosia sitting there. But there was nothing. "Baby girl? Where are you?" she said. Louder now, the cat replied. She was clearly somewhere close at hand.

"Oh, come on! Come out now!" She could hear her, so why couldn't she see her? It sounded like she was under the bed and yet she wasn't. She had to be hiding under the duvet, right inside the cover, that would explain the muffled sound.

Grabbing the quilt she yanked it off the bed and started to peel back the cover. Nothing! Theodosia was not inside.

"Meow! Meow!" Monica could hear it quite clearly, it was definitely coming from the bed. She got down on her knees again in one final bid to spot the kitten and it was then that she noticed the ragged flap in the base of the bed.

Examining it more closely she could see that the tweedy covering of the bed had been scratched until finally a hole had developed. Lifting the flap she peered inside, and there sitting amongst the springs was Theodosia, looking slightly irritated at being disturbed. Her deep blue eyes were round with expectation and her short lilac tail wrapped neatly around her feet.

There was no doubt about it, she had been a very feisty kitten. Would she really be willing to go through all that again as Patty had suggested? But then, as with many seeds, once they are planted they begin to grow.

Chapter Eleven

It would have been easy for Monica to dismiss the notion of getting a kitten as one of Patty's dim-witted ideas, but something about it wouldn't quite leave her. Maybe it was simply the thought of having a new life in the house. There had been so much sadness, so much that she wasn't able to do anything about, and now this could be one little piece of joy, totally under her control. She could choose it.

She flicked aimlessly through an old copy of *The Stage*. On one page was a young man she and Trevor had worked with a couple of years ago at Stratford, but his name had completely vanished from her mind, Josh or James? It was something like that. Lovely boy, so respectful...... Irritated by her ridiculous moth brain she put the paper down and picked up the phone.

After a couple of rings Trevor answered.

"Hello," he said. "Fred Karno's Circus, how may I help you?"

Monica laughed. "Going well then, darling?"

"Marvellously, absolutely wonderful, if you like total chaos."

"Look, I won't keep you if it's all going to hell in a handcart, but what do you think, shall we get a kitten?"

"What? What for?"

"Well, company I suppose. Now I'm at home I'd like something exciting to happen."

"Exciting? Well, I suppose you can do what you like, but wouldn't you be better off getting a dog? It would get you out of the house"

"Theodosia would loathe it and anyway, can you see me in green wellies and a padded gilet, exchanging pleasantries with the other dog walkers and swapping stories about what hilarious things little Bronte or Co Co have been up to?"

"No, but I can see you in a padded cell if you go on like this, hiding away there. It's just not you. You need people, Mon. Don't get something that will keep you at home even more. And what if you decide to come back to work?"

"That is very unlikely. I can't even remember that lovely young man's name we worked with at Stratford a couple of years back, let alone a whole script."

"Who, darling? Look, I can't remember everyone I've worked with; it doesn't mean anything."

As the conversation had gone on, Monica realised just how much she liked the idea of a new kitten and just how disappointed she would be if she didn't get one. Frustrated by her husband's lack of enthusiasm she said, "Please, Trevor. It would be so nice, all that zooming around. It would be fun!"

"Mmm, if you say so. Well look, if you're dead set on getting another one, go ahead. I've never been able to stop you doing anything once you've got a bee in your bonnet. And anyway, I've often thought Claudette had a point about Theodosia, and two cats being company for each other. The thing is, where will you find one? On the internet?"

"Oh God, Trevor don't be ludicrous. You know I hate damned computers. No, no, those cat magazines must still exist, the ones with all the little ads in the back. I'll do it the old fashioned way. I'll do some ringing round, someone will have kittens. I don't care what colour I get, do you?

"Look, Mon this is your department. You grew up with them, I didn't. Just try and remember all the stuff Claudette told you when she had them."

Monica laughed. *"Yes,"* she said, adopting her mother's way of speaking. *"My sweet, when you go looking for a cat there are only certain things you can do. Yes they must be healthy and yes they must be friendly, but after that…..it is up to them, not you, it is they who choose. Don't think too hard, Cherie, you will get the cat you are meant to have……"* Her speech trailed off and suddenly Monica found herself crying, tears rolling one after the other down her cheeks. It was the realization that she would never hear that voice again.

"Oh, Mon darling, I'm so sorry, I have to be away. You could really do with me being home…," said Trevor, hearing the emotion in her voice.

"Now look," Monica said, pulling herself together. She had to be brave for Trevor, he couldn't be worried while he was in a run. "I'm fine, it's just how it is sometimes, but I'll be all right in no time. Please darling, don't worry. You get back to work. I'm a kept woman now, can't have you slacking."

It wasn't one of her best performances, but it was enough to persuade Trevor that she would be fine. Sometimes she wondered if she would be fine ever again. Trevor signed off as cheerily as possible. They both knew they were pretending. Monica put the phone down and went immediately to find Theodosia, she needed to bury her face in the soft grey fur and weep.

Afterwards, feeling weak and strangely fragile Monica decided she couldn't face a trip into the village today. They probably wouldn't have what she was looking for. *Country Life* and a few women's magazines were all they seemed to stock in the tiny newsagents cum post office. She knew she would need to drive out to the supermarket on Monday, so she would try there.

The thought of the supermarket filled her with gloom. When she was at work she hadn't really been an organized shopper, they had had a very ad hoc arrangement, sometimes eating out, sometimes just getting something on the way to work. And once Claudette had moved in they had never worried about food, she took care of it, seemingly able to produce good food at whatever time of day and night they arrived home. But now she needed to plan. Being a housewife was one part of her retirement that Monica didn't relish.

"Well, then," she said, taking Theodosia's narrow little face between her hands. "What shall we do? I can't look for a kitten just yet, so I must think of other things."

Carefully placing the cat in her seat, she got up and went in search of a gardening book she had seen in Trevor's study. Despite Patty's dark misgivings about germination Monica still liked the idea of growing something, seeing it start as a plain brown little seed and blossom into something beautiful.

Taking the book from the shelf, she sat in Trevor's chair and began to flick through the vibrantly coloured pages. After a while she realised that she wasn't looking at the book at all and a memory of one of her old drama teachers came to her:

Mr Metcalfe would tell his students, "Now, whatever you do, for the next ten minutes, I don't want you to think about a purple spotted horse." And of course every last one of them could think of nothing else. The kitten had now become Monica's *purple spotted horse.* Try as she might to concentrate on the beautiful blooms in front of her, 'like a strong spring released,' her mind kept returning to the cat.

The study door squeaked slightly as Theodosia pushed her head through the gap and worked her way into the room. Monica watched her elegantly sashay her way across a patch of sunlit rug. They really were the most beautiful creatures, almost supernatural. Frost points, they were called in America. What a pity we didn't use that here, so much more descriptive than lilac.

"Theodosia," she crooned, "come and see Mummy." The cat paused for an instant, stared at Monica with round, blue eyes and then continued on her way; she had a different plan in mind. Jumping up she landed delicately on the printer in the corner of the room and settled down for a nap.

Independent souls, thought Monica. That was why she loved them so much and why Claudette had loved them too, they didn't follow anyone else's rules they just *were*.

Next to the printer was Trevor's computer. A blank forbidding presence that Monica usually avoided. Trevor had insisted that she learned the basics, like sending emails, looking up information, etc. but she really didn't feel comfortable with it. Things would just vanish from the screen for no apparent reason, and sometimes it seemed to do nothing at all so she got impatient with it. Phone calls were so much easier than all this technology.

However, today she felt an irresistible urge to walk over to it and type in Siamese Kittens. For a while she sat staring at it until finally she gave in. What harm could it do?

She switched it on and waited patiently whilst it went through all its annoying little stages, screens fading in an out, with various logos on them until finally it played, what Monica called, its "little I'm ready tune."

Excitedly she typed in the words and waited. 1,230,000 results! Now, this was exactly why she didn't like the computer. What could she do now, there were pages and pages of it? Pictures of kittens, stories about kittens, and something horribly headed "Preloved Siamese for Sale." It all seemed too overwhelming. How could she find a kitten amongst all this?

Then a heading caught her eye. About half way down the page was something called UK Cat Breeder Directory. Hastily she clicked on it. At the top right hand side was a little box for searching. Monica typed in Siamese and waited. There was still a huge list to wade through but at least she had narrowed it down. Her search had begun in earnest.

Page after page of beautiful little bat eared kittens gazed out at her, page after page of beautiful cats surrounded by trophies and rosettes. Little faces all needing to be loved. In one way she found it ineffably sad. What would happen to them all? At least she could help one. There had to be one that was meant for her, however, every time she found one she liked, it was in Fife, or on the Isle of Wight. Did no one breed kittens in Oxfordshire?

Impatiently Monica paged and paged. She knew Trevor would have laughed at her. There was probably some awfully clever way of finding just what she wanted, but she would just have to do it the hard way.

Eventually, with her eyes aching and her patience almost exhausted, she spotted a local number. It was over toward Little Rollright somewhere, but close enough. Lorelei Siamese. Feeling almost smug she clicked on a link and went to the home page.

Lorelei Siamese: *Based in the very heart of The Cotswolds we have been breeding beautiful Siamese for over thirty years. We are GCCF registered and all our cats are fully inoculated and insured.*

We occasionally have kittens available to the right homes. Please email or ring to discuss.

Chapter Twelve

It's odd that of all the words and names that we see in a lifetime, we never know which ones are going to become familiar to us or even be significant to us. Most just pass through and are never seen again while others stay and become very important indeed. For Monica, Lorelei Siamese was about to play very special part in her life.

She sat staring at the words on the screen for a while, trying to garner as much information as possible. Did they sound friendly? Did they sound like they only sold cats for showing? And did "occasionally" mean they'd have any at the moment? There was only one way to find out. Monica cleared her throat and rang the number.

After several rings the phone clicked over to a pre-recorded message welcoming her to Lorelei Siamese. Disappointed, she was about to put the phone down when a voice broke into the recording,

"Hello! Hello. I'm here. This is Laura speaking. What can I do for you?"

"Oh, hello. My name is Monique Pinto, and I was wondering if you had any kittens at the moment?" She always used her stage name when she wanted to impress.

"Oh, I see. Well as a matter of fact, we do have some just now."

Monica immediately noted the accent, it had to be Edinburgh. She would have known that slightly refined "afternoon tea" tone anywhere.

"What is it you're looking for? Showing? Breeding?"

"Oh, no nothing like that. I just want a pet."

"Ah, I see. Well now, have you been owned by a Siamese before?"

There was something in that tight schoolmarmish voice that made Monica feel a little nervous and on the back foot, as though she had to prove herself. She found she was gabbling away about Theodosia until eventually Laura cut in....

"Well, all that sounds fine, but I'd have to meet you first of course."

"Sorry?"

"I'd have to meet you, before you see the babies. You see, I don't let everyone have my cats, I have to be sure. What I'm saying is, I can't guarantee I'll let you have one. Not everyone who walks through my door goes home with a kitten."

Slightly insulted by this remark Monica said coolly, "Well, I can assure you, it would have an excellent home with me. I have a five bedroomed….."

"Any other animals?" Laura butted in, dismissing Monica's testimonial.

"No, just my Siamese."

"Uh huh, good, good. Did you have others with her."

"No, just her."

"I see."

That was clearly the wrong answer, because there was a long pause of consideration before Laura spoke again.

"Well look, all I can do is invite you over. We'll see if we suit one another and then we'll go on from there. So, you can get directions off the website. Shall we say tomorrow 2 o'clock. What was your name again? Monique, did you say? I'll put you in the book. Cheerio for now, then."

It wasn't often that Monica lost control of a situation, but today she had. She didn't even know what sort of kittens Laura had. Colour, sex, age, nothing. All she knew was she had an appointment tomorrow, when she may or not be allowed to see them.

Part of her felt angry at the way things had gone. After all, she was the potential customer, but she also knew that if she wanted a kitten, she would have to swallow her pride and abide by the rules. Turning to Theodosia, who had been watching her closely from Trevor's printer, she said, "What a cheek! As if Mummy doesn't know how to look after a new baby."

Theodosia let out a huge yawn, showing her two front fangs and an expanse of pale pink tongue. Clearly she was unmoved by Monica's indignation.

"Well, I shall just have to be patient, won't I? What shall we do with the rest of our day?" Reaching over to the cat she began to stroke her soft velveteen ears. "You'd like a friend, wouldn't you? It must be terribly boring for you, here by yourself with just Patty for company each morning."

Theodosia curled more tightly into a ball and deftly tucked her ear away from Monica. She needed her sleep. Taking the hint Monica got to her feet. Having a kitten around would certainly liven things up, but that couldn't be all. Trevor was right, she did need people. She went back into the living room in search of her list of possible activities.

Book Club was crossed through. Below that, it said horse riding, that was a possible. She remembered having to sit on a horse quite a bit in a production of *The Scarlet Pimpernel*. Learning to play a musical instrument? Too old. By the time she got to Grade 4 she would be eighty. Dance class? No, too energetic and probably full of young women in Lycra. The few times during her career she had been asked to dance, it had always been a struggle.

Re-train? Now that would be something, begin a new career. The phone suddenly rang and startled her from her reverie. Theodosia chattered in annoyance from the study.

Monica answered the call suspiciously. Trevor would ring her on her mobile, who would this be?

"Hello," she said.

"Hello, I hope you don't mind, but I got your number from a mutual friend, Patty Galton. My name is Sally. I run the Alms House Theatre group in the village."

This statement astounded Monica. Why would Patty pass on her number to the local amateur dramatic group?

"Yes," she said, cautiously.

"Well, Patty told me you are at a bit of a loose end, and we were wondering if you would like to come along and use some of your experience to help us?"

Monica took a deep breath. She was both annoyed with Patty and insulted at the same time…… AMATEUR dramatics! What had Patty been saying to people in the village? That she was all washed up? So desperate that she would join anything? Setting her face into a beatific smile she said as serenely as she could,

"Well, Sally, it was Sally, wasn't it? Thank you so much for your call, but I don't really think I would have time to attend. And as Patty has no doubt told you, I have recently decided to take a break from acting."

"Oh what a pity, although we weren't going to ask you to act, we were hoping you would direct for us."

"Well, as I said, I'm taking a break from all things theatrical. Thank you anyway. Goodbye now."

As soon as she ended the call, the fixed smile fell from Monica's face. Amateur dramatics? What was Patty thinking? She would have it out with her in the morning. God knows what else she had been saying. She might have a call from the local bring and buy sale next, to see if she could man a stall for them on Saturday, if she had nothing better to do.

She tried to stay calm and return to her list of things to do, but somehow the call had shattered her concentration. After seething inwardly for a minute or so, she managed to pick up her thread. Yes, re-training, that might be the answer. Studying for a whole new career, but in what field? Definitely a profession, not just a job. She wasn't good with blood, so that discounted anything medical. How about Law? She had played a barrister a number of times and after all it did call for a certain stage presence and a way with words.

Obviously she wouldn't go back to university with all those young people. Just the phrase "mature student" made her cringe. No, she would study from home. The Open University perhaps? She'd heard that it was much better these days, and no staying up until 4.00 a.m. to listen to strangely bearded men droning on.

It was definitely an appealing idea. She imagined herself in a wood panelled library somewhere, surrounded by heavy, leather bound law books.

She would find out about it. If she was honest she didn't know where to start. How did one get onto a course in the first place? Well, for now it was enough to know what she wanted to do. She'd talk to Trevor about it, and about the kitten, although maybe she wouldn't confess she was going to go through some sort of interview before she was allowed to have one. And what about Patty? She couldn't have Patty volunteering her services for all sorts of odd things, could she? That needed to be nipped in the bud.

But for now she had a plan. A new kitten and a new career. Happily she made her way to the kitchen. Maybe she would plant those seeds this afternoon, a trip out to the garden centre would do her the world of good.

On hearing the kitchen door open, Theodosia jumped down from her spot in the study and followed Monica with her cat siren set on high volume…. Reee-ow, reee-ow! Kitchen equals food.

Chapter Thirteen

Monica's afternoon spent exploring the garden centre had exactly the effect she had been hoping for. It was too cold to spend too much time in the outdoor section but, as she was happy to wander around inside soaking up the oddly comforting mix of warm, green growing smells, scented candles and coffee, she felt at peace.

Its air of gentility worked wonders for her soul. She felt much more mellow. Even her irritation with Patty had begun to fade. She also realized that she knew absolutely nothing about plants or gardening. A life spent acting didn't leave room for much else.

Optimistically she browsed the seed display. Lined up in their brightly coloured envelopes they all looked wonderful to her: red, yellow, blue; little paper packets bursting with life. She carefully selected some very traditional flowers, and some wallflowers and scented stock, the ones that reminded her of time spent with Claudette long ago.

Those summer days spent in their little back garden in Kent. Claudette with her brown, bare feet and tangled dark hair, a country girl, unfettered and uninhibited. She was not like the other mothers in the street with their click clack heels, smart coats and shiny handbags. There was always a wildness about Claudette, a freedom that never left her, even into old age. Claudette was a free spirit.

And now here Monica was, pottering around a garden centre like any other provincial housewife, admiring twee knickknacks and imagining cottage gardens. Claudette would have laughed at her and called her 'lady nose in the air,' of that she had no doubt.

When she had finally made her selections Monica made her way to the till. As she waited in the queue it occurred to her that there would be nothing to see now, just a few dormant seeds in tidy green trays. Near the entrance on her way in, she had noticed a display of winter pansies, already planted up on a plastic Grecian urn. Impulsively she slipped out of the queue and picked one up and took it with her. She would have some colour now, something bright, a happy bright splash of purples and yellows, colours that hinted of the end of winter.

The following morning Monica put her pansies out next to the front door, so that she would see them as she came and went. She had no idea what she would need to do with them, but it couldn't be that hard, could it?

Her next challenge was the seeds. Carefully she spread newspaper on the kitchen work top, sprinkled some compost into a tray and squinted at the instructions on the back of the first packet. All this was closely followed by a wide eyed Theodosia who had never seen activity like this before, and a tray full of earth was sure to attract any cat's attention.

Cautiously Theodosia tapped the seed tray with her paw and then extending her long neck and sniffed the damp compost. It was very small for a litter tray, so she looked questioningly at Monica, somehow managing to make her whole body a lilac question mark.

"You'll see, darling," said Monica. "There will be lots of lovely flowers."

At this point Theodosia stepped into the tray and tried to manoeuvre herself into position.

"NO! Theodosia. NO! Stop. No. Get down!"

Quickly lifting her clear, Monica placed the cat on the kitchen floor.

"It's not your litter tray," she said.

Confused the cat let out a plaintive meow, and clearly rather offended, she wandered out of the kitchen with her tail held high.

Relieved, Monica went back to read the packet of seeds. As she was still trying to decipher the little pictures of rain and sunshine, Patty arrived.

"Morning, Mrs P... oh!" She looked at the newspaper and the tray filled with compost and winced. "Oh dear, you're doin' your seeds, I see," she said.

"Yes, I want a nice display in the summer. I've put some pansies out too, by the front door. Did you see them?"

"Very nice. I'll leave the kitchen till last then, shall I?"

"Patty, before you go," said Monica, rubbing the compost from her hands, "I had a phone call yesterday from Sally something or another. From the am drams."

"Oh aye," said Patty, noncommittally.

"She said you gave her my number."

"Yes, I did. I didn't think you'd mind. My neighbour, Mary goes to it, does little plays and so forth. I thought it would be right up your street, now you've nothing much on."

For a moment Monica didn't know what to say. She had felt incredibly angry about it yesterday, but today most of that had subsided and she just wanted to make her point.

"Look, Patty. I don't mean to be rude, but I'll find plenty of things to do, and they won't be anything to do with acting. I'm having a complete change. I may not even go back to it, and I don't want you volunteering me for things."

The two women looked at each other for a moment, Patty sensing she had done the wrong thing, but not really understanding why. It all seemed quite plain to her. Monica was an actress and that was the place to act.

"Well, now," she said, slowly. "I must say, I think that's a pity. I do really. I wouldn't like to see you give up acting altogether, it would be such a shame. I always think God gives us these gifts for a reason. It's a proper vocation, you've got there. I've always wanted a vocation myself, but it never happened. Now my Cousin Audrey had one. It was her dream to go abroad and take up a missionary position."

Monica's annoyance drifted away and she started to giggle. The thought of straight laced Patty's cousin wanting such wanton a thing, was irresistible. "Missionary position," she said. "Couldn't she have done that in this country? Oh dear, I'm sorry, Patty."

She put her grubby hand up to her watering eyes, as laughter erupted.

"I'm sorry, I'm sorry. It just sounded so funny," she added. After the misery of the last few days, it felt wonderful to laugh.

"She were very religious, were Audrey. I don't see that's a laughing matter. I don't know that she did any good being out there in Brazil. It still looks terrible when you see it on the telly, but she would have done her best. She was like that."

"Yes, of course. I'm sorry, Patty. I'm sure she did." Monica looked hard at the seeds on the table, willing herself not to laugh.

"Anyway," said Patty looking, crestfallen, "I'm sorry I put my foot in it. I were just trying to help."

Something about her gloomy demeanour struck home with Monica and she felt instantly guilty for having raised the subject.

"I know you were, but I *have* taken on some of your advice."

"Oh yes?"

"I'm going to look at a kitten later on this afternoon, over at Little Rollright. Lorelei Siamese.

"Oh, now," said Patty. "That is something. Will you be fetchin' it home with you? Shall I find a box for it to sleep in, poor little scrap?"

"No, I don't think I shall be bringing it home. This is just a chat, today."

"A chat? What is there to chat about? You want a kitten, they've got a kitten. That's it, in't it? You just choose the one you like."

On the face of it Monica was inclined to agree, but she said diplomatically, "Well, I don't know, Patty. I suppose they have to be careful these days"

"I can see that, I suppose, there are some right odd people about. I saw one at the station yesterday, all covered in tattoos, and I bet he'd never even been to sea. No, I can't say I blame them, what with you bein' an actress and all."

With that Patty opened the store cupboard and pulled out the vacuum cleaner.

Monica watched her trundle down the hall, with the hoover trailing behind her like a reluctant metal dog, and she sighed. Patty was not the most tactful person in the world, but she meant well.

After lunch, with the seeds safely tucked away in slightly over damp compost, Monica turned her mind to the kitten. Patty had left for the day, and Theodosia was pretending to be asleep in the lounge, whilst carefully watching everything with just a slit of an eye.

What did one wear as a prospective kitten owner? Dame Edith Evans always started with the shoes, but in this case, what were the shoes? Nothing too smart, or she would look house-proud, nothing too casual or it would look as though she wasn't taking it seriously. Country chic? Tweed and leather boots? It certainly was tricky and she had to really feel the part to do well at the interview. Interview! What was she thinking? This woman wanted to sell her a cat, didn't she? Why was she so worried? It was nonsense. She would dress as she pleased.

Having selected a black roll neck sweater and black jeans, she looked in the bedroom mirror. Perfect. Just a little bit feline, but still very much her. Just as she was about to leave the room and go downstairs, she paused, opened a drawer and took out a small gold brooch in the shape of a cat. It had been Claudette's. Well, it could do no harm, could it?

On the drive to Little Rollright, she tried to tell herself that it didn't matter. If this bloody woman didn't like her, she could go to hell and she'd find another breeder. Who was she to judge? However, as she got closer to her destination she realized that rejection would hurt just as much as losing a part to another actress. Ridiculous? Maybe, but it was in her, something she couldn't control. She had to succeed.

As she drove along the wintery lanes, her mind turned to Theodosia. How would she really feel about a new cat in the house? Before she was able to dwell on this the sat nav advised her that she had 'reached her destination'. Slowing down she saw nothing, just an anonymous piece of lane. But then, hanging on a gate she spotted it, a metal sign swaying slightly in the wind. The words *Lorelei Siamese,* and *Welcome* were written in large curly writing, whilst below them sat a painting of an elongated and very stylised Siamese. Carefully she got out of the car and unhooked the gate. At least the sign was welcoming, if nothing else was.

Following the path she eventually came to what looked like a very large cottage. On the doorstep stood a small plump red haired woman dressed in a sweatshirt, which clearly bore the same logo as the sign at the gate.

Before Monica even had time to switch off the engine, the woman had left the doorstep and walked swiftly over.

"Monique?" she said. "I'm Laura. Welcome to Lorelei Siamese. If you'd like to follow me, I'll give you the tour."

For a strange moment Monica felt as though she had turned up at a tiny Highland distillery somewhere and was about to be walked through the whisky making process. She quickly got out of the car and followed her efficient little hostess.

At the back of the main cottage building were a series of wire pens. Peering in Monica could see very little and began to wonder why she was out here in the cold, looking at empty pens.

"My stud boys," announced her guide. "You won't see much of them today because it is rather chilly. They much prefer to be in their accommodation, which is kept at a constant 26 degrees, for their comfort."

As they passed quickly through, one of the cats let out a huge raucous meow and appeared from the little box-like structure at the back of the pen.

Without even looking up Laura said, "Oh yes, Rafferty, we can hear you. Now, away back to your bed and I'll be out to see you in a wee while. Visitors! Rafferty. Visitors!"

Whisking on, Monica found herself trailing behind like a bewildered child as her hostess marched through a series of twists and turns between the pens and finally arrived at a white UPVC door.

"This is the main office. We'll take tea and then I'll show you the play room and the nursery. Any questions so far?"

Monica dumbly shook her head. This was not at all what she was expecting, and she was beginning to doubt that she would even get a glimpse of a kitten today.

Chapter Fourteen

In the impeccably tidy office, a floral china tea set was already laid out on a large wooden tray.

"Please, do take a seat," said Laura. "Do you take sugar and milk?"

As her hostess busied herself with the tea, Monica looked around the office. With its tasteful décor and furnishings, it was more like a plush consulting room than a cattery. On each of the walls were beautifully photographed portraits of cats, some with trophies next to them, all looking incredibly regal and elegant.

Catching her gaze, Laura said, "My Imperial Grand Champions."

"Beautiful," said Monica.

"Now," said Laura in a business like tone. "You are here because you would like one of my Lorelei kittens. Well, as I explained on the phone, it is not just a case of popping in and choosing one. Despite what you may have been told, we breeders are not in this for the money. Were that the case, then we would certainly have chosen the wrong business. I pride myself in breeding healthy, well balanced, confident kittens and I spend a lot of time and energy making sure that they are. And so you will understand if I say I won't let them go with just anyone. I have invested a lot in these little lives and it's part of my job to see that they go to the right homes. So, that being the case I hope you won't mind if I ask you a few wee questions about yourself, your home, etcetera."

This really is like an interview, thought Monica. *How can you be interviewed about a cat?* But she smiled and nodded.

"Well, to begin then, are you *in* most of the time? I won't have them left all day while people go off to work. It's not fair, Siamese are sociable, they hate solitude."

"As a matter of fact I have just retired from acting, so I shall be spending quite a bit of time at home," said Monica.

"Uh, huh!" said Laura seemingly unimpressed by her interviewee's unusual career. "And you wouldn't mind if I did a few calls, just to check you were there?"

Monica shook her head.

"Good, and do you have another Siamese? I seem to recall you saying that you did."

"Yes, I do. Theodosia, my lilac point."

"Photograph?"

"Sorry?"

"Do you have a photograph of Theodosia with you?"

"Ah, no I didn't think it would be…."

"No matter, you can email it over to me later. I just want to check she looks happy and healthy."

Monica was feeling more and more on the back foot under this onslaught of questions.

"And you have a vet, I take it, for Theodosia? If you leave me his details I'll ring and check with him that you come in regularly for vaccinations etc."

"Erm, yes, I do have a vet." Monica's agitated brain began to let her down. What was the name of the vet? She had been with him for years! Why had his name slipped away just when she needed it?

"And who would that be?" said Laura, looking at her sharply. "I'll just make a note of the practice name."

Feeling herself flush with red hot embarrassment Monica said, "Oh, my goodness. I'm so sorry, I appear to have gone blank. It'll come back to me, I'm sure." Marvellous! Now she looked really suspicious.

"Right then, so how long have you had Siamese? I want to be sure you are quite used to the challenge they bring."

"All my life. My mother had them before I was born, I'm quite used to them."

"So they were your mother's choice? Not yours?"

"Yes, but I like them too."

"I see, and who looked after them when you were touring etcetera? I take it you did tour, that seems to be the way with acting?"

"Yes, of course, but my husband was there, and my mother would help a lot too."

"Uh, huh."

Another uh huh. Monica wasn't convinced that that was altogether a good thing.

"Now then, breeding plans. I had a gentleman here last week that was planning to take one of my kittens, he said for a pet, but I found out he planned to breed from her. So I showed him the door and made sure all the other breeders in the area were wise to his little game too. I won't have it. A pet is a pet. A breeding queen or stud is a different matter."

"No, no. No plans for breeding," stuttered Monica hurriedly.

"Good. I would ask you to sign a document to that effect, if you have one of my kittens."

By now Monica was beginning to think she would receive an application form in the post and then be called back for a second interview.

"Boy or girl? Point preference? And anything else you would like to say at this point?" said Laura, looking squarely at her.

Sensing this could be make or break, Monica mentally steadied herself. Taking a deep breath she prepared her performance.

"Laura," she began, carefully uncrossing her legs to appear more at ease than really she was. "I love Siamese," she said in a measured tone. "I have spent my whole life with them, I love everything about them. As to colour or sex, I have no preference; to me they are all equally wonderful. I have no desire to breed, abandon or neglect them, merely to give them a good life. I will look after them and most of all I shall love them. Beyond that I don't know what else I can say to convince you."

Laura sat back in her chair and put her pad down. "Well now, Monique, you have just used the magic word."

Monica raised an eyebrow. "Magic word?"

"Love. That is the most important thing you can tell me. It's not how big your house is, how much money you have, or even what you do for a living. What's important to me is that you love my babies. If you love them, then everything else follows."

"Well, I will," stated Monica, sensing victory. "I adore Theodosia and I'd do anything for her."

"Very well," said Laura, taking a sip from her cup. "Would you care to see the kittens today? I have a litter of seals just now. As you have a girl already, you might like to look at the boy. There's just the one male, but he's a heartbreaker already. Drink up your tea and we'll go through."

Feeling enormously proud of herself, as though she had just passed a particularly tough audition, Monica dutifully drank down her tea and prepared to pass into the inner sanctum of Lorelei Siamese.

Laura opened a door at the back of the office and led her down a short corridor, the walls of which, were covered from skirting to ceiling in rosettes and certificates. "Cat shows!" she said, seeing Monica's interest. "Run out of space, especially for rosettes. They always give you rosettes."

Beyond the corridor Monica could make out a huge open room, at the end of which, was a large

Aga range and scattered about were various climbing frames and equipment for the cats. The cat room!

"They'll be having a nap just now," commented Laura. "In the bed with Mum. She's a champion, their mother, Imperial Grand Champion, Lorelei Black Tulip. I call her Belle."

Walking into the room Monica felt that same frisson she had felt when about to go on stage, the butterflies chasing around in her stomach and right up to her throat.

And then she saw them, curled up in a plastic bed. A dark brown cat and five tiny cream coloured kittens all tucked into her stomach. She had forgotten just how tiny they were as babies and a little gasp escaped from her lips. On hearing the sound, the mother cat opened her almond shaped eyes and fixed them with a confident stare. The absolute blueness of her eyes caught Monica completely off guard, a gorgeous sapphire colour set in a dusky dark face. There was something almost unearthly about her. One of the kittens blinked up at them. Its dark little pansy face full of sleep, it licked its nose and quickly settled down again.

"That's one of the wee girls; she's going to Essex," said Laura and then, "Hello, Bellie Belle. Can we have a wee peek at your babies, then?"

The cat made a short chirruping noise and began to lick her brood.

Expertly Laura reached in and gently picked up one of the wriggling kittens. "She's an excellent mother," she commented. "Now this one is the boy.

What do you think? I've been calling him Big Chap, but you could soon change that."

It was beginning to sound more and more like it was a done deal to Monica and with a slightly shaking hand she reached out and touched the kitten's face.

"Oh, he's beautiful," she said, putting her finger on the tiny triangle of dark fur just above his nose. "Just beautiful."

The kitten raised one small paw and pushed her finger away.

"Leave my nose alone!" laughed Laura. "Would you like to hold him? He probably won't stay long but you are welcome to try."

As Monica took the wriggling, warm kitten, she realized that apart from Theodosia, who had been a gift, she had always gone along with Claudette to view kittens. Claudette had always chosen them and settled them in back at home. This time it was up to her.

Feeling strangely daunted by this idea she held the little cat gently and looked down at his tiny angular skull and huge bat ears. She wondered, would this really be her kitten?

The little warm body wriggled and tiny claws appeared poking out of the front paws. From the bed his mother let out a small meow. "Oh, that's it!" commented Laura. "He's had enough of that. He wants down. "As if to confirm this, the mother cat let out a short yeow sound. She was watching her kitten closely.

Carefully Monica placed him on the floor and instantly he raced off, skidding across the wooden flooring and pouncing on what seemed to be an old sock.

Monica could tell that he wasn't the least bit interested in her. She had been hoping that there would be some sort of instant bond, that she would know he was "the one" but the kitten happily skittered about on the floor with his sock, without so much as a backward glance at Monica.

She tried to remember how her mother had chosen kittens, but all she could think of was Claudette with her reading glasses perched on the end of her nose, holding up each kitten and looking into its little face. No doubt she had some eccentric theory about them, but this didn't help Monica.

"Why don't you sit down over there and see if he comes to you?" suggested Laura, perhaps sensing her disappointment.

Monica sat on one of the tattered chairs. Clearly it had been loved by many kittens over the years and now its tapestry like covering stood up in little bobbles, where a thousand tiny claws had plucked at it.

For a while the kitten continued with his own focused little game and then suddenly he dropped the sock, padded quickly over and jumped up on Monica's lap.

At first he sniffed about, stopping now and again to investigate an interesting smell on her knee, or sleeve, and then he settled. Looking totally relaxed he lay across her lap and started to chew on

Monica's gold bangle. Her heart melted. This was her boy.

"There," said Laura. "He seems to have taken a shine to you. I thought you'd get on. He's so laid back, that boy. At the moment he isn't reserved, so if you like him I'll put you down and you can have him in about three weeks. I'd expect you to visit once a week until he goes home with you. Fair enough? And of course I have a few more checks to do before I finally commit. Now, let's give him back to Mum and I'll show you their Daddy, my stud boy, Lorelei Atticus Catticus. Now he's a lad an half, that one."

Chapter Fifteen

Later that afternoon, as Monica drove home through the darkened Cotswold countryside, she tried to keep all the vivid images of the day in her mind: the tiny cream kitten with his brushing of colour, his huge, beautiful father standing proudly in his pen, and the unblinking blue eyes of his dainty, watchful mother.

It was like an enchanted world. She had to admit she hadn't been keen on Laura's brusque manner when they had first spoken but now, seeing her there, amongst her cats, she could understand why she was that way. They were her treasures, her beauties and she didn't part with them lightly. Laura's Siamese babies meant the world to her and Monica felt that, even if she did adopt the little male kitten, he would only ever be on loan from his ferocious "mother."

She decided that as soon as she got in she would email Laura with the information she had asked for. At least she could appear efficient even if she didn't feel it. She still couldn't remember her vet's name and even more annoyingly she realized that she had had his details with her in her address book all along. Her brain really wasn't functioning properly these days. And what was the other thing Laura wanted? The vet and? There had been a lot to take in but even so, she knew her memory wasn't up to scratch. She would have had all that sorted out in her mind in seconds in the old days.

Feeling suddenly tired, she tried to concentrate on the kitten. All being well he would be coming home with her soon and Theodosia and he would be a wonderful little family. It wouldn't matter about her memory then. She didn't need to perform for the cats, they would love her whatever her failings.

Not for the first time that day she felt very conscious of her mother's absence. What would she have thought of the "new baby"? Would she have approved? Would she have looked into his face and seen something Monica couldn't? It was so hard choosing without her decisive, impetuous mother at her side. Claudette would never even see this kitten, and that hurt. Perhaps she should have chosen a girl and called it after her mother? But it was too late now, her boy was coming.

It was early evening when Monica finally reached home. She had spent more time at the cattery than she had planned and Theodosia was not impressed. At first she pretended to be asleep in the chair before grudgingly stalking across the lounge and curling herself around Monica's legs and chattering up at her. Abruptly, she stopped and sniffed. Opening her mouth in a sneer she pulled in the smells emanating from her human.

*Strange cats! Why did she smell of strange cats? What **had** she been doing?*

The look on Theodosia's pale grey face was one of utter disgust and Monica quickly decided that if she didn't want to be sniffed reprovingly all night, she would have to change her clothes.

Having changed out of her traitor's garb she went straight to the computer. She got out Laura's card

110

and typed in the address. Should this be business like, she wondered, or friendly?

Before she could decide she noticed a new email. Clicking on it she was surprised to see it was from Laura, sent just after she'd left the cattery. It said:

"Thought you might like a photo of The Boy. He is the one in the middle, looking straight at the camera. Don't forget to forward vet information and photograph of Theodosia.

Kind Regards

Lorelei Siamese."

Relieved to have something to go on, Monica began a reply. It was difficult to get the tone right and even more difficult to find a good picture of Theodosia. In most she had bright red demonic eyes, or if she was being held by someone, it looked like they were trying to strangle her.

Finally she decided on a half decent one, then finished her concise little message and pressed send.

Clicking back to Laura's email she found herself gazing at the photo of the kittens. There was her prospective new boy lolling right in the middle of his sisters and looking directly into the camera. Fearless and confident. Monica liked what she saw, a proper little character.

Just then Theodosia wove her way around the study door and wandered in. She looked questioningly at Monica for a moment, before letting out a long wailing meow. It was almost as though Theodosia knew she was up to something.

Whenever Monica toured, Theodosia had always known days before she had even started to pack, and now she sensed something was about to change. Reassuringly Monica closed down the computer and swept her up into her arms.

"There's nothing to worry about, darling," she said. "It's all going to be fine.

Next morning as Monica inspected her seeds for signs of life, Patty came rumbling into kitchen like a tank, dragging her vacuum behind her.

"Mornin'," she said. "How did you get on, then? Did you get one?"

"Sorry?" said Monica, distractedly.

"A kitten! Did she let you have one?"

"Oh, yes. Well, I think so."

"You think so? Did she not say?"

Turning to look at Patty's frowning face, she said, "Yes, yes I'm sorry, Patty. Yes, she did. I am getting one. A little boy, in about three weeks."

"Good, that'll brighten things up a bit. And what does Mr P think of all this?"

Monica smiled. "Mr P" had responded as he always did when faced with one of her obsessions; he gave in gracefully. He really was a lovely man, and she loved him dearly. Perhaps she should name the kitten after him?

"Oh, you know. He doesn't mind," she said.

"No, well I expect he had no choice. Anyway, I'll get on. I thought I might clean the airing cupboard out this morning, it was full of fluff last I looked. The postman's been. I'll leave your letters on the chair, shall I? One with a cheque in it, a bill from the electric and a leaflet about a choir."

With that Patty wandered off, leaving Monica to contemplate just how her cleaner was able to glean so much from her unopened post just by carrying it in from the hall.

Having convinced herself that her seeds were doing nothing at all, Monica picked up the bundle of letters. It was just as Patty had said, but something about the leaflet caught her interest.

It was somehow so cheerful. Printed in reds and pinks it showed photographs of happy smiling singers, all looking like they were having the time of their lives.

"Have fun! Sing for pleasure and social interaction." It said. "Come and join us. Friendly local group. No auditions."

She stood for a moment, looking at the leaflet. She had dismissed a choir at first, after all, she wouldn't be centre stage would she? But perhaps it would be rather nice to be safely buried amongst others for once, no real responsibility for the performance, and this did look like fun. She imagined herself belting out songs at the top of her voice and not caring one jot how she sounded.

Why not try it? She was still looking for ways to meet new people, wasn't she? And she had to do something while she was waiting for the kitten to arrive. True, she had planned to start her new career, but with her memory being what it was and the kitten needing attention, she felt she could afford to put it off for a while. She would just concentrate on living and enjoying herself.

Since Claudette had passed she hadn't really felt alive, just strangely numb and as though most of her being was filled up with sadness, with just a little bit of life left on the surface. But now it was time to go out into the world and try new things. A new chapter.

"Do you still use this black towel? Or shall I wang it out?" said Patty breaking into her optimism. She was at the kitchen door waving the towel in Monica's direction.

"No!" said Monica. "It was a present from the company when I played Lady Macbeth. Look, they had it embroidered, 'To our wonderful Lady Black Death!' See!"

"Oh," said Patty. "Doesn't sound very pleasant to me. But if you want it."

"Patty. What do you think of this?" said Monica, holding up the choir leaflet. "I thought I might go."

Peering at it Patty said bluntly, "Can you sing?"

"Well I can carry a tune and it says they don't mind. It sounds fun."

"Well, I don't see why not. Singin's all the rage now in't it? That little skinny chap keeps going about starting choirs all over the place. I told you to join one ages ago. It does you the power of good. I love to sing, me. I never miss Songs of Praise."

"Really? Do you sing along to it?"

"Well, I do, but not when my Ray's in. He says it reminds him of when his father was in pain with his phlebitis."

Chapter Sixteen

"Alto or soprano?" said the steely haired clipboard lady. Monica was standing in the slightly chilly main room of the village community centre and she hadn't been prepared for such a technical question. She thought she would just go and sing along with everyone else, but Mrs Clipboard seemed intent on making things dull.

"Oh, I don't know," said Monica lightly. "I haven't really sung anything for years. Can I say neither?" she smiled, hoping to break the ice.

"I'll put you down as an alto, then," said "the gatekeeper."

Around her, ladies were gathering in little groups, chatting and looking at various pieces of paper. From where she stood, the paper looked suspiciously like sheets of music. Proper music! What did she know about music? Looking a little more closely she was relieved to see that not all the ladies had music. Perhaps they would be more like her, just along for the fun of it?

Mrs Clipboard clapped her hands together sharply and called,

"Jeremy will be with us shortly, but in the meantime can we have sopranos over here and altos here. Thank you, ladies. As quickly as you like."

Feeling like she was in a prisoner of war film, Monica found herself almost standing to attention. She felt as though she was on parade waiting for the commandant to arrive. No one said a word.

"Well," continued The Clipboard. "While we wait, why don't we do our loosening exercises?"

Now this was something Monica did know about, she had been doing it since drama school. Obediently they all began to rotate their shoulders and shake out their arms, letting all the tension go. This felt like home.

"Let's get those muscles relaxed!" encouraged their leader as they shook and stretched. "Open yourselves up."

However, before they could all loosen themselves any further, the main door swished open and a slim middle aged man rushed in. He reminded Monica of old illustrations of Jack Frost. A thin faced dart of a man, with pointed, angular features.

"Good Morning, ladies," he said, as he made his way swiftly to the piano in the corner of the room. Slipping on a pair of very thick glasses he started shuffle various music books. "Thank you, Joan," he said.

While he was busy, his assistant and chief clipboard operator started to hand out sheets of paper to everyone. "A new piece," she said solemnly to each person as she passed along. It was as though she was bestowing a blessing. *A new piece, and may God go with you,* thought Monica.

Yes, it was as she thought, real music! All sticks, dots and blobs. But she could still follow the lyrics,

117

couldn't she? To her relief it was quite a modern tune. An Adele song, in fact. She had the CD at home. This seemed a lot more hopeful, she'd had a horrible feeling that it would be all hymns and Handel's Messiah. Hallelujah!

Seeing Monica looking a little perplexed, the long, straight, strip of a woman standing next to her glanced over her shoulder and said, "Do you read music?"

"No," smiled Monica. "I'm afraid not."

"Well, I don't know how you expect to cope, then," she replied.

Before Monica could reply to this unexpectedly sharp little barb, choirmaster Jeremy started to play. It was a very crisp introduction and much slower than Monica had been expecting.

"Now," he began, "I shall quickly run through this, just so that you can hear how the lyrics fit." Then, in an odd high pitched, slightly tremulous voice, he began to quaver his way through the first verse.

Monica felt a powerful urge to laugh, but looking around her, she saw that the rest of the choir were all gazing intently at him while he carefully enunciated each word and earnestly nodded at the end of each line. Burying her giggles she tried hard to concentrate on the song.

But the combination of his reedy voice and the excruciating faces he was pulling got the better of her. Hurriedly she feigned a coughing fit and tried to focus on something sad. It had always worked on stage.

"Sorry, sorry," she whispered to the ladies nearest to her. "Annoying cough, sorry." Feeling calmer she looked down at her sheet music and tried to catch up with everyone else.

When he finally got to the end, Jeremy was obviously very pleased with the result and beamed at them. "Now, Ladies. Joan will take over at the piano and we'll try it, shall we? Thank you, Joan." He leapt out from behind the piano and prepared to conduct them.

"Are we ready? And …. *When the rain is blowing-in yourrr- face.*"

With his frenetic energy, piercing eyes and jerky arm movements he looked like some sort of mad scarecrow puppet. Instead of concentrating on the music Monica was instantly transfixed. What a performance! No actor she knew could have replicated those movements, they were so very peculiar.

And then, "Stop! Stop! Stop!" he yelled, pulling himself up into a human pinnacle of irritation. "No, you're lagging. Let's start again. And..."

This time, making a conscious effort not to look at him, Monica gave it her all. Singing with great gusto she was delighted to find that she could hear her voice above everyone else's. It really did stand out. Perhaps she had a more powerful voice than she thought? After the third verse, Jeremy stopped them all again.

"Look! Ladies can we at least try to sing the right notes! Someone is way off. Please concentrate! And again."

Monica had an awful feeling that he was talking about her and so she decided to tone it down a little. For the next run through she sang in a much quieter voice and hoped nothing would be said.

At the last note Jeremy was still looking pained. "Well, let's leave that one for now, shall we, and move on to an old favourite: *Bridge Over Troubled Water*."

As Joan began the distinctive piano introduction, Monica looked over her neighbour's shoulder for the words. They had only got as far as "When darkness comes," and Jeremy erupted again.

"Stop! Stop! You are garbling. I want to hear the words cleanly, cleanly!"

It was intense. Not the sort of sing-along fun she had imagined at all. And there was no talking between songs, just fervent preparation. Where was the fun? Where were the happy rosy faced singers on the flyer? This was not what she had in mind. This was more serious than a lot of the plays she'd been in. It was supposed to be a little local choir, not the Crouch End Festival Chorus.

Feeling a little irritated Monica decided to carry on and see if things improved. But as they progressed through one mournful song after another, the teacher chided them constantly. She had worked with some picky directors in her time but this man was ridiculous.

"Sopranos, you are a disaster! What are you doing? Come on, we've done this so many times, you should be able to sing it in your sleep."

They began again. It sounded fine to Monica. Everyone came in at the right time, everyone knew the tune. What else was there?

"I'll have to stop you there!" said Jeremy. "Has anyone actually practiced this at home? It sounds awful. I can see we will have to have extra rehearsals. Joan, see if the hall is free on Saturday morning, will you?"

This felt more like a punishment, than a hobby. Why were they all so serious? Now they were getting detention. Did nobody actually enjoy the singing, just for its own sake? And then, her questions were answered.

Tapping sharply on the top of the piano, Jeremy stopped them all dead in their tracks.

"This is a shambles!" he bellowed. "We only have weeks before our Christmas Choir Festival in Bicester and you still all sound dreadful! I can't even begin to imagine how your carols sound!"

And there she had it. This would never be the fun, happy get together she had hoped for, because this was serious, deadly, deadly serious. It was all about performance.

No matter how innocently things began they never stayed that way did they? Sooner or later the egos crept in and sooner or later people wanted to show off what they could do, to impress others, to say 'look at me'.

Monica knew this probably better than anyone else in the room. After all, she had spent her life performing, standing in cold rehearsal rooms and being shouted at, but that had been her job, her career. That had been to entertain paying customers. This was not. This was simply about being a big fish in a little pond and it wasn't for her. She wanted something with no pressure at all, something she could go along to and sing her heart out for a couple of hours, then go home and forget about it all.

As the choirmaster continued to berate his followers, Monica looked around her at their serious faces, all intent on chasing their few minutes of glory, and she knew she had to walk away.

At the end of the rehearsal, as the ladies neatly filed all their music away in their colourful folders, Monica made her way quickly to the door. She didn't want Jeremy or Clipboard calling her over for a 'little chat,' gently suggesting that perhaps she wasn't cut out for being in a choir. Part of her wanted to laugh, but part of her felt, that unless she found something to do, soon, her world was in danger of becoming as small as theirs.

Chapter Seventeen

Feeling more than a little let down by her experience with the choir, Monica sat in her favourite chair, chewing on her morning toast. Her mood was decidedly jaundiced. What on earth, she wondered, did retired people do? When she had been working she didn't seem to have a minute to herself and she would often had little fantasies about what she would do if she had more time. She would find herself dreaming of a more genteel way of life, full of art and culture, being surrounded by like-minded people. But where were these people?

When Trevor had warned her that she would miss her old life, she hadn't really believed him. After all she had never thought of herself as being defined by her profession and yet without it, she had almost lost who she was. Was she just an actress? Just someone who inhabited different people but was actually nothing herself?

It was a horrible thought and yet here she was, hopelessly looking around for something to belong to, something that would give her an identity of her own. So far things had not really gone according to plan. People seemed very reluctant to welcome outsiders and after mixing with theatre people for so long everyone else seemed a tad colourless and dull. She really was struggling to find something to do, life was passing her by. There were now more years behind her than in front and she needed to find a life for herself before it was too late. What she needed was a purpose.

As she finished the last of her toast, she heard Patty come in through the front door. Strangely, she felt almost glad to see her and called out, "In the lounge, Patty!"

A few moments later her cleaner stomped in.

"Mornin', Mrs P. You all right? You look a bit browned off, sitting there all curled up."

"Oh, you know. It's a miserable morning and I'm just feeling my age a bit."

"Oh, well. That's the trouble, isn't it? None of us getting any younger, are we? Before I came out this morning I had a phone call to say that my sister's friend, Sylvia has just passed away."

This wasn't the cheery conversation she had been hoping for but Monica said, "I'm so sorry to hear that. Had she been ill?"

"No, she'd been fine. Well, I say that, but she had a big operation a few years back and after that, she'd never really been what you'd call alright since. It left her with permanent stomach on the chest, you see?"

Monica forced herself to not ask the obvious question and said instead, "What a shame. Good health is so important. If you have that, nothing else really matters."

"Oh, I agree. It's a shame though, because poor Sylvia never really had much going for her. Very plain girl she were, she always reminded me of Spencer Tracy in *Bad Day At Black Rock*. Something about her eyes, I think. Anyway, how was your choir?"

Seeing an opportunity to change the subject Monica said, "Oh, it wasn't really my thing. I don't think I'll be going again."

"Oh dear. Are they that lot who sing outside the library sometimes? They always look like they've lost a shillin' and found a tanner to me. Ah, well at least you've got Christmas and the new the K.I.T.T.E.N to look forward to".

"Why are you spelling it out, Patty?"

"Well, out of consideration really. I don't want to offend Theodosia, do I? Look at her there all curled up peaceful. She hasn't a care in the world."

Monica looked across at the tranquil Siamese, sleeping peacefully in a pool of wintery sunlight on the window ledge. There was not one ounce of tension in her body. It was as though she had simply melted there.

"Oh, Patty! She'll love having a kitten around. It'll liven her up a bit. By the way, I shall be going to visit him again soon. The breeder insisted on it."

Patty raised her eyebrows skyward, but didn't comment.

"Once a week. It's a condition of me having him,"

"My goodness, that's a bit much, in't it? It's like going to church to hear the banns read when you want to get wed."

"She just wants to make sure I'm committed, I suppose."

"She's the one as ought to be committed, in my opinion. Carrying on like that over a kitten. Oh well, the kitchen won't clean itself. Give us your plate and cup, I'll teck it with me and meck a start."

Monica watched her go and did wonder for an instant if Patty wasn't right. Perhaps it was all a bit over the top, maybe she should find another breeder who didn't make you sign a contract in blood? But having seen that little furry baby once, he already had his paws on her heart. Now she was determined to jump through any hoop Laura cared to set for her in order to bring him home.

Feeling restless she stood up and went over to Theodosia. Carefully she ran her hand over the sleeping cat's soft flank and down its tail. Then taking one of the delicate leather padded paws in her hand, she gently squeezed. There was something irresistible about those feet but had Theodosia been awake she would have snatched it away immediately. They were not for mere humans to fondle.

It was still early but Monica felt an urge to ring Trevor. She really wished he could pop home now and again, but the travelling back and forth took it out of him these days and so he preferred to stay in London. She would make sure she went to visit him before the kitten arrived. They could spend an afternoon wandering around Covent Garden like they used to do. It would be so lovely to see him. Perhaps she could even go today? Just on the spur of the moment, it would be fun.

They had often spent long periods apart over the years, it went with the job, and as they were both in the business they understood. But now it was different, one of them was left behind with nothing much to occupy her time.

She selected Trevor's number and pressed Call. A very sleepy voice answered.

"Hello." Monica could tell from the husky sound to his voice that she had woken him up.

"I'm sorry, darling. Were you sleeping?" she said.

"No, it's fine. I should be getting up soon anyway. It's my day off today, I don't want to waste it."

"So how is the play?"

"Oh, it's a joy! We're at that lovely phase, when everyone has hit their stride, they know what they are doing and everybody has settled into their roles. It's marvellous. And the audiences have been wonderful, Mon, so appreciative. You should see Jenny. Well she IS Queen Victoria. I feel like I should bow every time I see her. We are all calling her Queenie."

Monica laughed. It was lovely to hear him so happy, but a little part of her felt a pang of envy. It wasn't her play, it wasn't her company, and it wasn't her applause.

"Good, good, I'm so pleased for you. Listen darling, I thought I might come down to see you, just for the afternoon. What do you think?"

"Today? That would be fantastic. Come, I'll meet your train. We can pretend we're Trevor Howard and Celia Johnson."

"I have so much to tell you about. I tried to join a choir yesterday, it was a total disaster! Oh and yes, the kitten. I must tell you all about the kitten. I have a photograph of him."

"Has he got a name yet, this kitten?"

"Well," said Monica coyly, "I was thinking of naming him after my favourite man."

"What, Ian McKellen?" said Trevor. "I'm sure he'd be flattered."

"No you, stupid. Trevor. It's a wonderful name for a cat, and I'm so grateful to you for being so marvellous about all this: me retiring, getting another cat. I just thought it would be nice to call him after you."

"Well that's very sweet of you, but I do think it would be a bit confusing, don't you?..... *Get out of the bedroom, Trevor. You know you aren't allowed in here*…. That would give Patty something to tut tut about. You can if you really want to, but I don't think the poor little fellow will know if he's coming or going. Look, we can talk about this later, just get yourself ready and text me when you are on the train."

"Well, what about naming him after your character then? John Brown," said Monica, ignoring her husband's request.

"John Brown?" sighed Trevor.

"Well he's a seal point, that's sort of brown."

"Mon, it's too boring. Theodosia and John Brown? It just doesn't sound right. Now come on, get ready. Think about it on the journey."

"Okay, okay, I'm going. Love you, see you later."

As Monica ended the call and bent to kiss Theodosia's nose, an idea came into her head. The cat twitched her ears irritably and settled herself into an even more comfortable position.

"What about Ghilly?" Monica said aloud. "John Brown was a ghilly! It's perfect!"

She immediately grabbed her phone and rang Trevor.

"Hello, it's me again. I have the perfect name. Let's call him Ghilly."

Chapter Eighteen

Christmas at the Stonehouse was an inconvenience that year. All Monica wanted to do was to fast forward everything to the new year, when they could all get back to normal.

Of course it was impossible to ignore it totally, it was everywhere she turned: special food, special cards, special presents, special, special, special! But Monica didn't feel special, it all seemed as artificial as the snow on the TV advertisements.

Grudgingly she had put a small tasteful wreath on the front door and twinkly lights across the hearth and that was the sum total of her decorations. The truth was her heart wasn't in it. If she was able to cancel it and move it to somewhere in the middle of March, say, she might have summoned up some enthusiasm.

She and Trevor had never really made much of Christmas, perhaps if they had been in a different line of business, or maybe if they had had children it would have meant more. But as it was they were normally both working right up until the big day, and then it usually felt like a rather pleasant long weekend.

She quite enjoyed the atmosphere at the theatre during the festive season though, people were out to enjoy themselves, they were generous with their applause and it suited her. She shared their excitement without having to get too involved with it herself. But even so, she was always secretly pleased when January arrived and things started to return to normal.

This year she felt she had an even bigger reason to wish it away: the kitten. As soon as all the festivities were out of the way she could collect him and they could start their lives together.

And so she endured the fuss, slavishly writing Christmas cards. She put the same message in each, she hadn't got the patience this year to personalize them all. She just wanted them done and gone in the post.

Her Christmas shopping became a military exercise. She did it in Banbury in one go. The women got perfume, the men got aftershave. All wrapped in store and ready to go. No imagination required, it was just ruthless and effective. Even Trevor's present was placed in a gift bag rather than the usual shiny wrapping paper.

But there was one shopping trip Monica was looking forward to. Shopping for Ghilly. The pet shop was completely overwhelming. She usually picked up everything she needed for Theodosia at the local shops, but this was on a totally different scale. Aisles and aisles of pet food, beds, toys, cleaning products, it was hard to remember that this really was all for animals.

It was also a shock to her to realize just how much she had relied on Claudette for organising things like this. Monica had always been the high flyer, the one that was able to dash off to the theatre and leave everyone else to it. Her mother would say 'Now, Choupette, off you go. I will be *fine. Go and use your talent as God intended. Your mind must be uncluttered, think only of your acting. Go, go, go.'* And Monica would leave without a second thought.

Claudette had always wanted her daughter to act, and had worked hard to make sure she did, seeing her through Saturday morning drama classes, endless amateur plays, and finally proper drama school. A little bit of Monica wondered if her mother had wanted to act herself and was living that ambition through her, but Claudette would never admit to such a thing and laughed it off with a casual, *'Me? Act, oh no, no, no!'* None the less she saw everything single play Monica was in, from her school productions right up to the RSC.

But now she was gone. For a moment as she stared at the multi coloured packs of kitten food laid out along the shelf, her eyes blurred with tears. Where did these overpowering surges of emotion come from? She could be feeling quite calm but suddenly sadness would rush over her and she was lost.

Reaching into her coat pocket she found a crumpled tissue and quickly dabbed at her eyes. The woman standing next to her glanced furtively across at her, and said, "Aahh, it's hard, isn't it? When you lose one? Especially this time of year. Still, you're doing the right thing getting a kitten. I've been through it myself." Then, squeezing Monica's arm reassuringly, she walked away.

For some reason, the notion of replacing her mother with a kitten seemed so ludicrous that she wanted to laugh. Claudette would have loved this little story. If only she could have told her.

Gathering her raw wits together Monica finally found the kitten food Laura had instructed her to buy and put it into her trolley. It was hypoallergenic, whatever that meant. Next on the list was a bed, he wouldn't want to share with Theodosia. The selection was huge and Monica immediately found herself drawn to a wonderful little four poster bed, complete with red velvet curtains.

She reached up and stroked its fur fabric pillows, it was like a prop from a very small set. But as she tried to imagine it in her home, a picture of Patty's scornful face came into her mind. As far as she was concerned, cats slept in cardboard boxes not reproduction Louis XIII beds. In the end she selected a much more sensible beige and brown bed with a fur trim. Patty couldn't possibly mind that.

As she wandered around looking at all the pet paraphernalia and listening to the sound system blasting out *Santa Claus Is Coming To Town* she began to feel a little bit like an expectant mother preparing the nursery. What else would this little boy need? When Theodosia had been a kitten, she had had a beautiful pink ceramic dish with mice and fish all over it, and so she was determined to find something like that for Ghilly.

After meandering fruitlessly along the bowls for a while, she decided to ask an assistant. She found one sitting untidily on the floor unpacking stock.

"Excuse me?" she said. "Do you have any bowls with pretty designs on them? I can only see plain ones on the shelf."

The plump young woman looked up at Monica for a moment. She had dyed bright red hair, a tinsel crown and what Patty would have called 'a rivet in her face'. "Bowls?" she said, slowly.

"Yes, the bowls. I wanted a patterned one."

"Well the bowls are there - on that shelf."

She had that peculiar way of speaking that Monica had begun to notice amongst young people, that odd midway pause, and then the last few words rising like a question.

"I know, but they all seem to be quite plain, I wanted a pattern. Do you have patterned ones?" she persisted.

"Sometimes – we do."

"Well, will you be having any in soon?"

"I don't think so - because - what happens is - people buy them."

Monica drew her hand across her chin. *Isn't that the rather the point of a shop?* she thought, but seeing there was little to be gained in continuing, she thanked the girl and moved on. She looked forward to the day when she too could be one of the lucky people who bought them.

As she was standing in the queue, and the Christmas music had worked its way round to the first tune again, she now had a trolley full of everything she could think of that a kitten might need. She ran through the list in her head: food, bed, litter, litter tray, toys, plastic bowls for water and food, treats. That had to be everything. As it was, she would have to sneak it all in so that Patty wouldn't give her one of those fish eye stares of hers.

She was almost at the checkout now, and something caught her eye. A whole section on oral health. Cat and kitten toothpaste and toothbrushes! Toothpaste? Brushes? Did people really do that? Brush their cat's teeth? How on earth did they manage that without serious injury. Feeling a little guilty she looked the other way. There were some things she wouldn't even consider attempting.

Outside in the car park as she loaded up her boot, a sudden rush of excitement came over her. This was it! Soon she would be bringing the kitten home. She tried to imagine him, all oversized ears and big feet, running around her house. Saturday 4th January. On her kitchen calendar it simply said *Ghilly*.

She had never had to visit a kitten before, and at first it seemed like a bit of an imposition but over the last three weeks they had built up a definite rapport and she liked to think that he now recognized her. It was amazing just how many changes she had seen in him. He was already looking more like a boy. There was an indefinable quality that she had noticed growing in his face, and whatever it was, it definitely made him male.

She hadn't told Laura about her choice of name yet. To her he was still Big Chap. Monica was just a little afraid that she would disapprove, and the kitten would need a new name. She had no plan B. She had become accustomed to calling him Ghilly in her mind, and it would be hard to think of him as anything else. To her it was the perfect name. A Scottish name for a cat from a Scottish breeder. But she just wasn't sure that would Laura would take it as a compliment.

The last time they had spoken on the phone Laura had said that his mother was 'getting a wee bit snippy with him.' At thirteen weeks old, he was ready to move on to his new home. "I've a feeling Belle will be glad to be shot of him," she had joked.

On Saturday January 4th she woke early with a splitting headache. The cold weather had changed overnight and the slightly warmer temperature had brought with one of her sinus heads. This wasn't how she had imagined it at all, she wanted to be on top form and with everything under control. She crept to the bathroom and took two pain killers. Her face looked washed out and dark under the eyes.

Well, the show must go on. She would just have to pull herself together. She had told Laura she would be there by nine, so she needed to keep moving. Theodosia shouldered her way into the bathroom and demanded breakfast. "Reeeee-ow! Reeee-ow!" she said, looking up at Monica with huge cornflower blue eyes.

This would be the last time it would be just her and Theodosia for breakfast. It was an odd feeling. Together they went down stairs and Monica put some food into the bowl. What would it be like this time tomorrow with two noisy mouths to feed?

As the Queen of the house tucked into her salmon and vegetable terrine, Monica went upstairs to shower and change. She had chosen her outfit last night so all she had to do was get into it. In the shower she held her head under the warm spray for as long as she could, desperately hoping that the pain would ease.

When she was finally up and dressed, she was pleased to see that she would almost pass for normal. She stood in front of the bedroom mirror and appraised her reflection. Not bad at all. She was wearing a pink blouse with a tiny kitten print design on it, which she had bought especially for 'kitten day,' and she was pleased with the result.

Her head was still pounding but at least it had receded a little so that she could concentrate on the job in hand. At 8 o'clock the phone rang. Panicking that this could be about the kitten, she tripped over the footstool on her way to answer it. Swearing she rubbed her shin and snatched up the phone. It was Patty. "Just wanted to wish you well with the kitten. I'll try and pop in later and see him, if that's all right?"

As Monica kissed Theodosia goodbye and went out to the car, she couldn't help but think fondly of her cleaner. She was an odd soul but her heart was definitely in the right place. She got into the car, looked inside her handbag once again to make sure that her cheque book was there, and slowly pulled off the drive.

It was a beautiful morning, the hard edge of winter seemed to have been blunted by the warmer temperature and there was almost a hint of spring in the air; it wouldn't be long before the snowdrops started appearing. Uplifted, and with her headache almost gone, she prepared to turn onto the main road to Rollright. *Ghilly,* she thought, *I'm coming to get you.*

For the next few miles she drove along in a bubble of contentment. This was the best thing that had happened to her in ages. A good, positive thing….. and then, like a neon sign lighting up in her head ….. it dawned on her that she forgotten to buy a cat carrier.

Her stupid, stupid moth brain had let her down again. She was heading off to fetch a cat, with nothing at all to bring him home in! At the next parking layby she pulled in. This was too much. She had spent ages in the pet shop, going over and over everything she would need, and yet an obvious thing like that had totally slipped through her mind and floated off into the ether.

But what to do now? She could phone Laura and ask if she could borrow a carrier. She must have a spare. Or she could turn back and fetch Theodosia's big white mesh carrier, which would be much too big for the kitten. She sat for a while as vehicles whizzed by, rocking her car as they passed. Somewhere the melancholy bleat of a lamb calling to its mother came to her across the air, and Monica felt utterly bleak.

In the end she phoned the cattery and lied. She said there had been a slight problem with the car and that she would be with her as soon as she could. Not for one moment did she consider telling the truth. Laura must never know just how incompetent she was. Fortunately all those years of lying for a living served her well and she did it with aplomb.

Wearily she turned the car around and headed home to fetch the carrier, and by this time her headache was back in full swing.

Chapter Nineteen

As Monica pulled into the now familiar drive of Lorelei Siamese, there was almost a sadness hanging over her. This would probably be her last visit. She had become quite fond of it but after today she would have no reason to come to this peaceful place, with its beautiful sleek cats and their ferocious Scottish mother? But, she told herself, at least she had the anticipation of bringing Ghilly home and all that entailed.

Within seconds Laura appeared at the door of her cottage, smiling broadly and raising a hand in welcome. She crunched across the gravel and opened Monica's car door.

"Well, then. The big day!" she said, bending to look in. "Shall we go and get your boy?"

They walked swiftly through the pens and into the main office. Here Laura stopped and motioned for Monica to sit down.

"Let's get the paper work out of the way, shall we?" she said, handing Monica a small folder. On the front was a picture of a kitten and in Laura's neat handwriting the name *Lorelei Black Prince*.

"Oh," said Monica. "You've named him…. I had…"

"No, no, that's just his official name, his posh name. I've registered him under that. But you can call him what you like. I just chose that because I'm working through Royals at the moment. The prince was born up the road at Woodstock apparently. So anyway, what will you call him? Have you had any thoughts? Of course some people like to have them a few days before they decide."

Taking a deep breath Monica said, "We're going to call him Ghilly. My husband is in a production at the moment; he's playing John Brown, Queen Victoria's ghilly, so we thought it was rather appropriate."

There was a pause.

"Very, unusual," commented Laura.

"You hate it, don't you? We can change it, I just thought it was nice."

"No, no, not a bit of it, of course not. It's those soppy names I can't abide, like snuggles and muffin. Makes fools of them. No, it's fine, and it has a nice royal connection. Ghilly, I like it. Now then, back to the formalities. In that folder you will find his pedigree, kitten guide, food requirements, an official invoice, his vaccination record and two papers for you to sign regarding neutering and what to do if you need to return him."

This all seemed very serious to Monica. She had imagined nothing more complicated than putting him in the car and driving home. She didn't remember it being like this at all in the past. Obediently she signed the papers and gave them back to Laura. Then, taking out the cheque book, she wrote in the agreed amount and handed it over. Neither of them said a word. It was almost like a secret transaction, as though money shouldn't really be involved at all.

"Well," said Laura, locking the cheque away in her desk drawer, "I think it's time we went to see him. I'll send the slip on to you in a few days, so you can register him as yours. Shall we?"

As the two of them made their way down the rosette lined corridor, Monica said, "Do you hate it when they go?"

"Of course, but that's the nature of the beast. I couldn't keep them all, and so long as I feel I have done everything I can to get them good homes, I'm satisfied. And anyway, most people stay in touch, you know, send me pictures, that sort of thing, and I see some at the shows, now and again."

As they entered the cat room, with its warm homely atmosphere, Monica was aware of little bodies darting around. It was the first time she had seen the litter so active.

"Making your sisters squeal again. You're a holy terror. It will be so peaceful around here with you gone," said Laura, immediately identifying Ghilly amongst the others. "Well now, Big Chap your mum is here, so let's get you ready."

At that moment Monica felt a horrible sense of guilt. She was taking this little boy away from the very heart of his family, away from everything he had known. This was his world and it was about to change completely. And there he was, playing with his feather and having no idea what was about to happen to him.

"Well, he should be fine," said Laura. The vet saw him yesterday for a final check. He's had his breakfast. I'd say he's raring to go. Now, have you brought a carrier with you? Silly question, I know, but you'd be surprised how many people forget."

Sheepishly, Monica made her way to the car without saying a word. When she went back to the kitten room she was surprised to find Laura holding Ghilly tenderly and talking to him.

"Okay, well here's your mum, now. So you just remember what I said and be a good boy, eh?" With that she kissed him on the head between the ears and popped him deftly into the carrier. "Right then, let's get going. I don't want to upset the others."

As they made their way outside, Ghilly began to panic and scrabble a little at the corner of the cage. This was proving harder than Monica had imagined. She began to feel like the evil Fairy Queen stealing away with a child.

Laura placed the kitten on the back seat and looped the seatbelt through the handle of the carrier. "I was going to have him in the front with me," said Monica.

"No, no, it's better like this, and don't be tempted to keep talking to him, it'll make him worse. Just let him settle in his own time. You have my number, so any problems, just give me a call."

It may have been Monica's imagination but she thought she detected just a hint of emotion about Laura's rather sudden departure.

With a final look over her shoulder at the wide eyed kitten, sitting forlornly in his oversized carrier, Monica started the engine.

"Off we go then. Let's go home, Ghilly," she said. The kitten replied with a plaintive but silent meow. It was going to be so hard not to say anything to him.

For the first part of the journey Monica kept glancing over her shoulder to make sure all was well. Occasionally, if he caught her looking, he would let out a loud squeak and stretch his neck in her direction. After a while, when it became apparent that this tactic wasn't working and she wasn't going to pay him any attention, he started to take an interest in his surroundings.

Carefully he sniffed every corner of the cage, taking in the strange scents, before managing to topple over onto the blanket as Monica turned a corner. Quickly getting up again he balanced himself again and, like a surfer on a choppy sea, began to learn how to move with the motion of the car and ride the bumps as they came.

After a while Monica became aware of another sound apart from her engine, she was sure she could hear purring. She looked at the little serious face in the mirror and was sure it was coming from the kitten. Why was he purring? And then she remembered when she was a child, one of their cats, a big chocolate point called Jean-Luc, would always purr on the way to the vet or when he was upset about something......'Listen, Monique," her mother would say, "he is whistling in the dark. It makes him feel better when he is afraid. So brave, my Jean-Luc."

Could it be that this little boy was toughing it out too, pretending to be fine. Monique felt a lump come to her throat and she longed to stop the car and hold him. With his little pale body and smudged dark, brown nose, he looked the very picture of vulnerability, and she knew there and then, that she had fallen in love.

She drove on, wishing the miles away. All she wanted to do was get home and cuddle him on her lap, and to begin being his new 'mum'. She knew they would help each other. After all the sadness of the last few months Monica felt she needed more love in her life. She had been feeling so old and lonely lately. Not having her mother any more had made her 'the adult' and she just hadn't been ready for it. It was ridiculous at her age, and she knew it, but she never had been very good at being grown up. She was much better at playing make believe, and of course she had been doing that all her life.

For the last part of the drive Ghilly settled down in the corner of the cage, tucked his tail over his nose and fell into a deep sleep. Poor little chap, he must be exhausted, thought Monica.

When she finally pulled onto the drive, she felt exhilarated. She was home. She could see that the kitchen light was on and guessed that Patty had popped back to wait for her. A few months ago this would have sent her into a rage, but now she just felt pleased. She would have someone to share this momentous event with.

As soon as she got out of the car and closed the door behind her, Ghilly woke and started to shout, his tiny pink mouth opening in a huge waaah!

"Okay, okay darling. Just a minute, I'm coming." She undid the seatbelt and pulled the carrier out.

"There we are, you're home now. Let's go in, shall we?"

With the carrier swaying unsteadily, she carried it to the back door and went in. Patty jumped to her feet.

"Oh, here he is!" she said. "Hello, puss." She bent down and peered into the cage. "I've bought you a tin of Whiskas."

"Hello, Patty. It's good of you to come back like this," said Monica.

"Well, I wanted to see 'im, didn't I, the lad? Has he been all right?"

"Yes, fine, I just couldn't wait to get here. Where's Theodosia?"

As she asked the question, a delicate lilac figure came around the kitchen door. Her confident walk and demeanour gave no indication of just what was about to happen.

A second later she spotted the carrier, her carrier. She sidled slowly over to it, pausing only to sniff the air as she approached and looked in.

"This is your new brother, Ghilly," encouraged Monica. "Isn't he lovely?"

Theodosia looked at the tiny fawn kitten and slowly lifted her face to look at Monica. In her expression, was utter devastation. Her Wedgewood blue eyes registered total betrayal and there was no doubt in Monica's mind that if Theodosia had been able to talk, she could have said,

145

"Oh my God, what have you done? What's this thing?"

Just then, Ghilly let out a huge spitty hiss, directed straight at Theodosia's face.

Chapter Twenty

"Well, now," said Patty, "that has put the cat amongst the pigeons, hasn't it? Madam here, doesn't like the look of him."

Monica stared down at Theodosia. Her tail was now fluffed up to enormous proportions and she was stalking slowly around the cage making the most awful gurgling yowls in her throat.

"She'll get used to him, I'm sure. It's just a shock to her," said Monica as brightly as she could.

In truth she wasn't at all confident that this was the case. She had never had two cats together before and Claudette had tended to get hers as kittens together. So this was a first for her, an older cat with a kitten, and she wasn't sure that she knew what to do. She wasn't really prepared for them to hate each other.

Theodosia jabbed a paw into the cage and took a swipe at Ghilly who responded by hissing even more loudly and retreating to the farthest corner.

"Why don't you let him out?" said Patty. "He's a sitting duck in there."

"What if they fight?"

"Well, you just keep hold of him and they can't, can they?"

Nervously Monica undid the top of the carrier and reached in for the kitten. He was so light, and as she scooped him up, she could feel his little heart fluttering in his chest.

"There," she said, cradling him in her arms and carefully stroking the serious little frown lines on his brow. "Don't look so worried, Ghilly, it's all going to be fine. She doesn't really mean it."

The kitten looked up at her with his blue solemn eyes and immediately began to struggle. He was afraid and panicking, and before she could grab him, Ghilly had slipped from Monica's arms, leaving behind him a set of vivid red claw marks on her wrist.

He bolted straight across the wooden floor in a scatter of feet and claws and scuttled under the sofa, closely followed by a sniffing, hissing Theodosia.

"Well, that's that, then," said Patty, disappointedly. "You won't see him for the rest of the night now. Our old cat, Tigger hid under the bed for a week once, after we took him to the vets. I'd best be off, now I've seen him. Good luck, then. I'll see you in the morning, Mrs P."

And with that she trudged down the hall and was gone, leaving Monica feeling utterly distraught. The whole beautiful vision she had been carrying around for weeks had vanished under the sofa. This was not going to be the happy little family she had imagined. Lowering herself to her knees she peeped at the kitten. There he was, hunched right at the back with his indigo eyes as round as plates.

Fortunately the space was much too small to accommodate Theodosia so she settled down to stare menacingly at him. Like a mouse in a hole, he was trapped.

Monica decided that at this point there was nothing she could do. At least the kitten was safe for now where he was. How she was going to integrate them, she had no idea. One thing was for certain, she couldn't phone the cattery and ask for advice. Not only would she be admitting defeat but in all likelihood, Laura would jump straight in her car and come and take Ghilly back.

Pensively she went to make a pot of tea. Just now and again these days she liked to make it properly in a tea pot. There was something almost therapeutic about the ritual of pouring the hot water in, clinking the china lid down and waiting. There had to be an answer to this. Perhaps Theodosia would change her mind and mother him? Or maybe Ghilly would win her over with his charm? As the kettle clicked, Monica tried her very best not to feel down hearted. After all it was early days.

Then a loud hiss and a crash came from the living room. Rushing in, Monica found that Ghilly had broken cover and was now streaking around the room with Theodosia in hot pursuit, both of them knocking anything that got in their way to the floor. She was just in time to see the kitten's bottle brush tail disappear under the sideboard before Theodosia closed in on him and once again settled down to watch her prey.

This was becoming a nightmare. Monica looked around at her normally elegant lounge. With books, papers, remote controls and pot plants scattered about, it resembled a dishevelled maiden aunt, who had just been manhandled. Slowly she began to put things back in place. This was not the happy event she had been looking forward to for the last few weeks. This was like an explosion.

By the time she got back to the kitchen all thoughts of tea had left her mind and she put the tea pot back in the cupboard. As she returned to the kettle with a jar of instant coffee, she was amazed to find Theodosia sitting on one of the kitchen chairs, glaring at her.

"Hello, darling. Why are you being so horrid to that little kitten, then? He hasn't done anything to you, has he?" she said, in what she hoped was a soothing voice.

"Reee-ow, yow, yow!" spat the cat in reply before turning, jumping off the stool and heading for her food bowl. Something in the way she flicked her tail in Monica's direction as she walked away, was more eloquent than a million meows. Theodosia had made her point.

Flopping down at the table with her mug of coffee as a comforter, Monica tried to stay calm and take stock of the situation. At least for the moment Theodosia was in here with her, eating biscuits, and the kitten was in the other room, hiding under the sideboard. And so nothing too terrible could happen. She took a sip of her coffee and decided this was just a typical opening night. It would all settle down in time and this would be a distant memory.

By the end of the cup, she was feeling a little more relaxed and hopeful. She decided to take the opportunity to wander into the other room and see how Ghilly was doing in his "mouse hole." But he wasn't in his mouse hole. There was no sign of him under the sideboard or the sofa. Slowly, Monica began to crawl about the lounge, calling, "Puss, puss, puss! Where are you? Ghilly?"

Seeing her on her hands and knees Theodosia came rushing in to help. She began by sniffing Monica's hair and trying to see what she was looking at.

"Theodosia, stop it. That isn't helpful. I'm looking for the kitten." Undeterred the cat continued to enjoy this unusual situation of seeing Monica so close to her own height and rubbed enthusiastically against her face with her wet biscuit whiskers.

"Darling, please!" said Monica, looking frantically under the armchair. She was now beginning to panic, Ghilly was nowhere to be seen. Feeling exasperated she picked Theodosia up and carried her into the hall. She couldn't cope with her "help" any longer. As soon as she closed the door on her, Theodosia began to scratch agitatedly at it.

Returning to her search, Monica tried to go logically from one end to the other, calling softly as she went. Now and then she could hear a little squeak but it was impossible to tell where he was. She reached for her phone and began to phone Trevor, he was always so calm when this sort of thing happened. But then again, he would be getting ready for the evening performance and it wasn't fair to bother him. This was her problem and she would sort it out.

"Ghilly!" she called, "Ghilly, Ghil!" Where could he be, it wasn't a huge room? And then she heard the tiniest muffled mew. This time it was definitely coming from the sofa and he sounded distressed. In an instant Monica realised that like Theodosia and the bed, he had somehow made his way inside it.

Anxiously she removed the cushions and groped down the back. Nothing! Then she began to feel along the sides, listening intently like a safe cracker. Not a bump, not a movement. Horrible thoughts began to rise in her mind: what if he had skewered himself on a spring or choked on foam or whatever it was stuffed with. Oh God, the poor little kitten, suffocating in there.

Sweat began to ooze from her skin as she imagined the call she would have to make to Lorelei. She had only had him for four hours. In desperation she turned the sofa on to its back and looked underneath. The arms were hollow and suddenly she knew what had happened. Steeling herself she looked up inside the arm, dreading what she might see - poor Ghilly wedged up there suffocated like a poor little chimney sweep. But there was nothing there, just the dark fluffy inside of the sofa.

Monica sat back on her heels and stared at her upturned furniture. Half relieved and half frustrated she let out a huge sigh. Her mother had told her to embrace the chaos, but this was purgatory. Where WAS HE?

At a loss, she sat and looked around the room. Everything was silent, but then she heard it, a scrabbling noise coming from behind the book case. Transfixed, she watched as a teeny pair of dark ear tips appeared, followed by a little pointed face.

Thank God! There he was. For an odd moment Monica felt that she was about to cry. Emotion and relief came over her in equal measures. Slowly she got to her feet, went over and lifted Ghilly out from behind the book shelf. Looking at the tiny gap he had managed to squeeze himself into, she pondered on just how difficult keeping tabs on him was going to be.

Gratefully she pulled him close to her face and kissed him. He was fine, he was safe and sound.

"Oh Ghilly," she said. "Don't do that to Mummy. I was so worried. Come with me and we'll find you some food."

As she carried him into the kitchen she heard a low growl coming from under the hall door. For now that particular crisis was over, but there would be many more to come, and she knew it.

Chapter Twenty One

Frustratingly, for the rest of that evening Ghilly continued to crouch under the armchair. As soon as he had wolfed down his food he had bolted straight back into the lounge and gone to ground again in seconds. After twenty minutes of coaxing, it became clear to Monica that he was determined to stay put and no amount of soft words and reassurances would lure him out. Reluctantly she opened the door to the hall and let Theodosia back in.

Like a diminutive lioness, she prowled into the room, whiskers pushed forward and with all her senses on high alert. There was an intruder in here and she would soon seek him out. Her eyes scanned the scene carefully before she made her way over to the armchair and growled a low throaty warning.

Monica was at a loss. Why did Theodosia hate him? He hadn't done anything apart from hide under the chair. Her beautiful Theodosia's face was shaped into a mask of mistrust and aggression. This kitten had clearly been a huge blow to her.

Disheartened and tired Monica decided that she needed food. Not wanting to leave the two cats alone together she hurried to the kitchen, tipped some cornflakes into a bowl, slopped on some milk and hurried back. Nothing had changed. Theodosia was still standing guard next to the chair with her face jutting belligerently toward the kitten. It was hard to see her Theodosia as an aggressor but she certainly meant business.

It seemed wise to Monica to station herself in the chair and use her legs as a barrier between the two cats. She decided that the best she could do for the time being was turn on the TV and hope that they both settled down. After ten minutes or so had passed she realized that she had no idea what she was watching. Every time the kitten moved, Theodosia let out a spiteful hiss and Monica jumped. Concentration was impossible. But persist she must, she had to ignore them. There was nothing she could do about the situation except hope it changed.

After a very long hour Theodosia finally hopped lightly up onto her lap, but instead of settling down as she normally would into a cosy sleep, she remained jumpy and watchful.

"Go to sleep, darling," said Monica stroking her gently. "Don't worry about what the kitten is doing, just go to sleep." But Theodosia was not going to be caught off guard and so all three of them sat in the all-pervading tension until the phone suddenly jolted them into life.

It was Laura. "Hello, there," she said. "Everything okay? Is the big chap settling in?"

Putting a smile into her voice, Monica went into to acting mode. "Oh, fine, fine, yes. No problem at all."

"And Theodosia, she likes him?"

"Well, early days, you know?"

"A wee bit hissy then? Not to worry, they'll sort it out between themselves. Of course, you'll be separating them tonight, I suppose?"

"Yes, of course," lied Monica. She hadn't considered sleeping arrangements, beyond them having a bed each.

"Okay then, I'll leave you to it. Just give me a call if you need me. Bye for now."

Monica put the phone down and felt absurd. That was her opportunity to ask for help and she was too proud to do it. Too proud to say she was hopelessly unprepared and was struggling to cope. Why was everything so difficult these days?

Separating them? What did that entail? Theodosia could go to bed with her of course, but what about Ghilly? He would have to be shut in the lounge......with a bed..... water.... a litter tray! Litter tray! He hadn't used it yet, he must need to go by now? How long could kittens hold on? He hadn't had a wee since leaving home that morning. Perhaps he was just weeing behind the chair?

Hastily she got to her feet and fetched the little plastic tray from the kitchen. It didn't fit under the chair! Poor little soul, he must be bursting by now. For a moment she was stuck. The kitten wouldn't come out and the tray wouldn't go in. What should she do? She crouched down and called to him. He responded by shuffling even further back into his hiding place and letting out a worried squeak.

As she stood up to consider her options for a moment, she saw that instead of just standing guard, Theodosia was now sitting amongst the litter.

A look of enormous satisfaction spread across her face as she produced a huge swamping wee, in the kitten sized tray.

Having deposited the soaking litter into the bin, wiped the tray and refilled it, Monica was in no mood for any more nonsense. It would be a relief to get away from the situation and go to bed. Feeling guilty she began to prepare. She deposited Theodosia in the hall, placed the litter tray, Ghilly's bed and small bowls of food and water near the chair and turned out the lights. That was that, she would begin again tomorrow. Perhaps they would be friends in the morning.

As she opened the door into the hall, Theodosia shot past her like a lilac bullet and had to be dragged away, protesting loudly. How could she be expected to sleep with a trespasser in her house? Monica struggled to carry her upstairs and as they reached the second landing, she broke free and hurtled back downstairs to sniff and claw at the lounge door.

Pulling herself up straight Monica went determinedly about her preparations for bed, ignoring Theodosia's scratching and squawking from below. As she went into the bathroom her phone beeped and a message from Trevor arrived.

Happy kitten day! Hope you are having fun!. Speak tomorrow. Xxx

"Hope you are having fun," she said aloud. She quickly sent a smiley face and some kisses. This wasn't the time to go into detail. Carefully she began to take her make up off, and told herself that she had to just get through this. The kitten was here now and it had to work. From the hall Theodosia let out a frantic blood curdling yowl and Monica pushed the bathroom door shut.

Eventually things went quiet and Theodosia pattered her way upstairs and into the bedroom. Usually she would have jumped up onto the bed without hesitation and settled down near Monica's head, but tonight she lay at the bottom of the bed curled in a tight ball. It wasn't clear if this was a protest or her way of being prepared to defend the room. Either way, Monica thought it best to just let her get on with it.

At a little after 3 o'clock Monica felt herself been pulled gently up to the surface of wakefulness by an unfamiliar noise. A sorrowful, insistent call from downstairs. For a moment she couldn't imagine what it could be and then, she remembered, the kitten. The poor kitten, she had intended to go down and check if he was all right, but the stress of the day had exhausted her and she had fallen into a deep sleep.

Her first instinct was to jump out of bed and rush downstairs, but a warning voice stopped her. When she was little and a new cat came into the house, Claudette would always forbid her kind hearted daughter from having them upstairs in her bed with her.

"Remember, cats are not like you and me. The night time is for them, the best time and they want to play. You, Choupette will be too kind, you will give in and play…..and then he will know that every night he can wake you up and you will play with him."

Was this what the kitten wanted? Attention and a game? Monica lay still and listened. The plaintive little mews made her wince. He was obviously very unhappy. Poor little soul, down there in a strange place, all on his own. He was probably missing his mother.

Perhaps she should just pop down and see. But then if he's fine, it would just disrupt things and he would have to get used to being alone all over again. What if it was just a ruse to get attention? Monica lay in the dark listening to Theodosia's tiny 'hamster snores' and wondered what she should do.

The kitten then found it's volume control, and went up in pitch, all at the same time. Monica sat up. What if he was stuck? What if he was really inside the sofa this time. Something about the soft plaintive wailing made her feel slightly alarmed. She got out of bed, slipped on her robe and went quietly out of the room, carefully shutting the door behind her so that the watchful Theodosia could not follow.

She went along the hall and cautiously opened the lounge door. Her heart began to beat a little more quickly at the thought of what she might find…… a tiny injured kitten, or worse?

Sensing no movement she flicked on the light. There was Ghilly, sitting right in the middle of the coffee table, gazing skyward with his angelic sapphire eyes, whilst all around him was in chaos.

The bed had been dragged across the room and one of Theodosia's toys was now floating tragically in the water bowl. Whether that was suicide or murder was hard to tell. Litter had been trodden to all four corners and into the rug, and a large damp patch was spreading ominously across the sofa.

Chapter Twenty Two

Patty stood in the doorway and looked sadly around the room. Monica had tried to tidy the most unpleasant bits away before she came, but Patty was clearly shocked by what she saw.

"Oh 'eck!" she said. "It were a kitten you had in 'ere last night and not a couple of wild boars? And what's all that on't rug?" Patty always became more northern when something displeased her. Standing with her hand on her hip and her mouth turned down, she couldn't have looked more disappointed.

"Yes, I know. I'm sorry, Patty. I think it may be litter. It all got a bit difficult and as I said, Ghilly had to sleep in here last night."

"So, she's really taken against him then, Madame Theodosia?" Monica nodded. "Oh dear. Well look, I'll crack on in here and you go and give them their breakfast. Food is always a good peacemaker, I find."

"Oh believe me, I've tried. They won't eat anywhere near each other. I had to resort to pushing the kitten's food under the chair to get him to have anything."

"Oh 'eck," said Patty again. "What'll you do with 'em?"

"Persist, I suppose, it's all I can do. Anyway for now, I've shut Theodosia upstairs and......"

Monica's mobile rang. It was Trevor.

"Hello, Mon, how is the new Pinto puss? I thought I'd have hundreds of pictures of him on my phone this morning."

Patty mouthed, *"I'll get on,"* and tactfully went out to the kitchen.

"Oh, darling I'm at a loss. They hate each other. I don't know what to do; it's awful. What if they never get on? What if I have to take Ghilly back?" she gabbled, relieved to finally hear Trevor's rich, comforting voice at the end of the line.

"Whoa, whoa, whoa, steady now," said Trevor. "They've only just met. You didn't like me the first time you saw me, did you? Give it a chance."

"Well, no I didn't, but I don't think Theodosia is about to be won over by his beautiful voice and charming ways."

"Well, what would Claudette have done? She must have come across this sort of thing."

"Oh, God, I don't know. She seemed to have a sort of magic with cats, almost as though she was half bloody feline herself. I don't remember any problems when she was here. She just seemed to sense what to do."

"Well, look, it's only the second day. You have to set some boundaries, show them how you expect them to behave, or they'll carry on being difficult.

Remember, Mon you are the human, you are in charge."

Monica didn't answer. Tears were welling up and emotion closed her throat momentarily. Finally she said, "Trevor, I wish you could come home. I miss you so much. I just feel so hopeless lately, everything I try to do goes wrong. I seem to make a mess of everything. I can't even handle a kitten. I miss Claudette, I never realised how much she did to keep things running smoothly for me. I didn't appreciate her enough. Oh God, I feel awful. Can't you come home for just a little bit?"

"Mon, Mon come on, sweetheart. You know I can't leave in the middle of a run, and it's going so well; they love my John Brown, and I love him too. I can't abandon him, can I? I'll ring you tonight after the show. Just try not to get upset. You know Claudette couldn't stand tears. As for the moggies, you just need to be strict with them. Show them how it's going to be. You can be bloody awe inspiring when you take command of a situation. So, come on, Mon….."

Feeling bolstered by her husband's praise, Monica smiled a 'brave' smile. "Yes, you're right," she said. "I can't let this beat me. It's just another challenge to overcome, isn't it? Claudette would tell me there is always an answer."

"Of course it is. Mon, you've faced worse than this, remember that production with Roger Brazier? Look, I have to get on, but I'll speak to you later. Now 'Cry havoc! And let slip the dogs of war!' All right?"

Determinedly Monica said her goodbyes. Trevor always made her feel better about herself. He was right, she had to move things on. They couldn't just stay deadlocked. She didn't want an upstairs cat and an invisible kitten. As if he had sensed her determination, Ghilly came cautiously out from under the chair. Bobbing his head as he came, he still looked on the edge of flight. But gradually as he realised there was no immediate threat, he began to explore, his outsized kitten feet treading softly across the carpet as he sniffed his way towards her. At intervals he found the odd piece of litter or thread that needed thoroughly inspecting and stopped to give them his full attention. Monica held her breath.

When he finally came within arm's reach she called out, softly,

"Ghilly, hello darling little boy. Ghilly come and say hello."

The kitten looked at her uncertainly for a moment before walking over to her. He meowed, revealing tiny pointed teeth and a pink tongue as his meow turned into a squeaky yawn.

"Hello, sweetheart. Can I pick you up?" Monica slid her hand under the cat's little rounded belly and pulled him up into her arms. He felt so delicate and light compared to Theodosia and his whole body vibrated with purring.

"Hello then, Ghilly. Aren't you a handsome boy? Now, what are we going to do to make friends with Theodosia, hmmmm?"

Patty carefully opened the lounge door and immediately broke into a smile.

"Aah, he's come out, then? Let's have a look at him." She made her way over and gently stroked the kitten's ears with one of her plump red fingers, "Like velvet," she murmured. "Hello, little lad."

"I'm going to fetch Theodosia in a moment," said Monica. "I think I need to take charge of the situation, be firm with them both. They really do have to get on."

Patty frowned. "In't it a bit soon? They can be awkward little devils. Best leave 'em to it, I say."

"No, I've made up my mind, this can't continue. Now, you hold on to him for a moment and I will go and get Theodosia. We'll introduce them properly."

Carefully Patty took the tiny kitten from Monica and cradled him maternally against her large bosom. "Hello, chicken," she said. "You're lovely, you are. Are you purring at me, are ya?"

Monica made her way upstairs, determined that this should be resolved. A repetition of last night could not be allowed. She hadn't told Patty about the wet patch on the sofa yet and goodness knows what else they would discover if the kitten continued to stay in the lounge overnight.

She found Theodosia sleeping in the spare room, her flank rising and falling peacefully. Monica sat on the bed next to the cat and ran her hand along its smooth back. "Wakey wakey, sleepy girl," she said. The cat stirred and blinked up at her. "Come on, we are going downstairs. I want you to come and say hello to Ghilly." She picked the drowsy Theodosia up and held her over her shoulder like a baby.

Before they reached the bottom of the stairs Theodosia had become very alert, as though she sensed what was about to happen. Carefully Monica pushed open the lounge door and went in.

As soon as the kitten spotted her he tried to escape from Patty's hold, wriggling frantically and digging in with his back paws. Somehow Patty managed to hold on and Monica advanced with Theodosia.

"Now then, darlings. Here we are. Let's be friends, shall we?"

Almost instantly Theodosia opened her mouth and spat pure venom in the direction of Ghilly, and followed it up with a hair-raising moan. The kitten didn't feel inclined to find out what happened next and so after a frenzied struggle he leapt from Patty's grasp and shot off like a furry missile.

Theodosia growled fiercely and jumped down from Monica in an attempt to follow him. But the kitten was so fast he had managed to fly up to the top of the curtain pole before Theodosia could reach him. He was now sitting, looking down at them with his ears pressed back to his skull and a ridge of fluffy cream fur standing up along his spine.

"Now!" said Monica, clapping her hands together. "This will not do. Stop this nonsense!"

Theodosia continued to prowl back and forth along the window sill yelling up at the terrified kitten, her fur bushed up and her wild eyes crossed in fury.

Monica had imagined that there would be a bit of hissing, a lot of sniffing and then, finally acceptance, not full all-out war like this. It was obvious there would be no way of getting the kitten down from the window until Theodosia had been removed, so once again she was shut out in the hall, and Monica went to find the stepladders.

Chapter Twenty Three

Over the next few days Theodosia became ostensibly an upstairs cat. It was just the very thing Monica had been trying to avoid. She had upset her existing cat and made life hell for the new kitten. Nobody was happy. The cats ate separately, slept separately, and hardly acknowledged the other's existence.

Thankfully, Ghilly seemed to have settled down a little. He hadn't tried to destroy the lounge again since his first night, and now only started yelling for attention once it got light. But still it was a very sad situation and despite Trevor's optimistic view, Monica couldn't see how it would change.

Sometimes Theodosia would pass the lounge door en route from the spare bedroom to the kitchen and glare in. She liked to check if the interloper was still there, and when she spotted him, she would let out a long, rasping hiss that could only mean 'stay away from me'.

Late one afternoon when Monica was sitting with Ghilly asleep on her lap, the lounge door creaked open and Queen Theodosia made her entrance. It was clear from the onset that she had had a change of tactics; today she would ignore the kitten, he was totally invisible, he didn't exist. She strolled across the room, sniffed nonchalantly at the bottom of the coffee table for no apparent reason and hopped up on the sofa, right at the other end of the sofa from Monica and the kitten, but in the same room and on the same piece of furniture. Could this be progress of sorts?

Ghilly was in a deep, deep sleep having spent an excited hour racing around the room without touching the floor. His batteries had finally run out and he had fallen into an exhausted slumber. He was now so still that it was almost impossible to see him breathing. He didn't even notice when Theodosia moved herself just a little bit closer.

Monica stared straight ahead and waited, almost holding her breath as she sensed the cat getting closer and closer. Eventually, she felt a warm, furry body snuggle in next to her hip and settle down. The two cats were now literally only a foot apart. She breathed a sigh of relief. Perhaps this could work after all? She would now be able to report honestly to Laura for once, instead of glossing over the truth as she had been.

For half an hour the three of them remained still, Monica willing herself not to fidget and break the spell. If this could become normal, or better still if they would actually curl up together, it would be wonderful. And then the phone rang!

Monica grabbed it straight away but it was too late, the harm had been done. Both cats had seen each other and had jumped off the sofa, Ghilly to hide under it and Theodosia to make her way to the kitchen as though that was where she was always intending to go.

The caller was Clara, making one of her monthly bids to try and tempt Monica back into acting. As ever, she was both ebullient and hectoring all at the same time.

"Spring is coming. You've had the winter off, now let me find you a new project, something to keep you occupied. Retirement must be so dull for you. Isn't it dull for you?"

Feeling slightly irritated by Clara's timing Monica said sharply, "I'm fine, darling. I have plenty to do. I don't know how I found the time to act. I couldn't go back to it now."

"Oh, surely there must be days when you miss it? Perhaps I could find you just a little something, just to keep you going. A little cameo, or a voice-over somewhere?"

"No, really I'm fine as I am. I'm enjoying my freedom too much to come back."

It wasn't strictly true of course, but she knew Clara of old. One small sliver of doubt and she would have been fixing up an audition, or a lunch to talk to 'some people'. She had to be firm.

"Okay, just thought I'd check. You know where I am if the mood takes you. Bye, Monique. Take care, darling."

Monica could imagine Clara putting the phone down and going to the next one on her list. *Monthly calls, Monique Pinto, tick.* She didn't mind, really. She knew she had made the right decision. An actress who can't remember her lines is a bit of a chocolate fire guard, and she was in no rush to be humiliated again. But even so, the calls always

170

seemed to unsettle her somehow, a strand from her old life pushing through into the present.

However, after that afternoon's mini breakthrough of two cats, one sofa, a very slow thaw began to take place, and over the following few days Ghilly and Theodosia could sometimes even be found in the same room. The older cat still refused to acknowledge the younger one's existence, but the kitten was a trier. He was still keen to be friends and he would occasionally walk right up to Theodosia in an attempt to rub his muzzle on her, only to have her hiss loudly in his face, whip herself round and trot off flicking her tail at him.

Some days were better than others. Sometimes Monica could get them to eat cooked ham together from her hand, and on others it was as difficult as usual and they became two very separate entities. One step forward and two back it seemed. All the time she could hear her mother's voice saying, "You will find a way. There is always an answer."

Despite all this, Ghilly was turning out to be the most loving little cat, not aloof or reserved in any way. He constantly jumped on things to be near Monica, often ending in disaster when he chose unlikely foot holds, but it was clear her adored her. His dark little face would gaze up at her and his whole being would resonate with purrs.

With his dusky face and his bright blue eyes, he was very different from Theodosia. She was all about shade and subtlety while Ghilly was striking and full of contrasts. His slim, dark legs seemed to be growing faster than the rest of his body, giving him an endearing, slightly gangly look.

As soon as Monica sat down he would arrive, walking about on her lap until he found the exact place to stand and be stroked. He was an absolute joy, which made it all the more hard to accept that Theodosia just didn't like him.

Monica's calls to Lorelei were becoming more and more difficult. Laura was very astute and so if she didn't report in, she would often ring out of the blue, "Just to check all was well". Monica found herself constantly emphasising how wonderful Ghilly was and how delighted she was with him but skipping over his relationship with Theodosia.

Occasionally Ghilly would forget himself and rub the length of his little body against Theodosia in a friendly greeting, and it was heart breaking to see him rejected, as inevitably he was. However, he never reacted with so much as a hiss. He just carried on…… being there. Monica tried to imagine how he must feel, coming to this awful place with such a nasty housemate, but if he was deterred he didn't show it.

That was the one consolation, Ghilly appeared to be happy despite his welcome. He just went about his life and let Theodosia get on with hers.

Theodosia, on the other hand was put out. She had taken this very personally. How could Monica have done such a thing? Betraying her by bringing in an outsider to spoil their happiness.

Monica was relieved that at least this show of disappointment was only external. Theodosia hadn't taken to her bed like some Victorian heroine or started losing weight. It could only be hoped that eventually she would come to terms with it and things would get better.

And then one glorious day, Monica returned from the supermarket and found a note from Patty on the kitchen worktop.

Careful how you go in the lounge. They have been curled up together all morning. Patty x

Her cleaner had been following the progress, or lack of it, avidly. Occasionally she would offer advice such as rubbing talcum on them both to disguise their smell, or putting butter on their paws, none of which seemed very sensible notions to Monica, and especially when it was suggested that they should be rolled up in a blanket together to transfer scents. Goodness knows where she got these theories, but she meant well, and so Monica did her best to take them with good grace.

Picking up the note she made her way very, very quietly into the lounge. And there they were, in the armchair. A large cat in a crescent moon shape and the downy youngster curled into her, both looking like little cat angels. Monica stood at the door and felt her heart lift. Finally!

Perhaps she could get a quick photo on her phone and send it to Trevor. But as she reached into her pocket, Theodosia opened one sky blue eye, and finding that she had an uninvited bed mate, she reached out with her paw and clonked him right on top of his head. A resounding *thunk* sounded as claw met bone and echoed in Ghilly's skull.

For a second he didn't move, and so to hammer home her point Theodosia boxed his ears with alternate paws and sent him on his way. This chair was hers.

But even so, this unlikely encounter was to be a turning point and an uneasy peace began grow between kitten and adult. A kind of forbearance on both sides.

Chapter Twenty Four

In March, spring came to The Stonehouse. In the garden waxy, green buds started to give everything a soft coat of pale green. Courageous young daffodils set their faces into the wind and tiny snowdrops nodded their encouragement. This was a season that Monica had always loved, a hopeful time, and this year she could actually enjoy it. Instead of rushing through it on the way to work she could take time and appreciate it all. Sometimes, in the past, the only way she had known the seasons were changing was by the type of flowers she had in her dressing room, but not this year; this year she would be out amongst it.

Some of Monica's seeds had managed to survive the winter despite her over enthusiastic care and they now looked like straggly little plants. They would soon need to be re-potted. And best of all, Trevor's run at The Lyric had finally come to an end and he would be coming home.

For the first time in a long time her heart felt lighter. So, as the March days began to get brighter, peace broke out at The Stonehouse. Monica felt as though she had survived a storm at sea and was finally sailing into calm waters.

As for Theodosia and Ghilly, they seemed to have come to some arrangement between them and although they were not close, they did manage to tolerate each other quite well. Theodosia still had days when she crept about like Mrs Danvers at Manderley, stalking the innocent and sending malevolent thoughts his way, but on the whole life was good.

For the time being Monica had decided that she wouldn't try and join in any more social activities. With Trevor at home, there would be no need and she still liked to keep an eye on the two cats, just in case.

Patty, however, didn't share her view. "You want to get out and about more. The weather's turning nice now. You don't want to be shut up inside."

Monica half wondered if Patty liked having the house and the cats to herself, and would much prefer her employer to be out of the way. But she was determined to do what she felt was right, and being around the cats until she felt confident they could be left, was what she intended to do.

When she shared her feelings with Patty they were met with an incredulous laugh. "You are joking?" she said. "Haven't you noticed how that little lad can take care of himself? He's got Madam's number all right. I were watching them the other day and she doesn't get the better of him very often."

"Well, I still think he's a bit young to be left with her for too long. You never know, Patty. I don't want to come home to blood and gore."

"Do as you please, but I still think it's like protecting the iceberg from Titanic, myself."

Whatever Patty's view, Monica knew that she still didn't trust the two cats alone. If things got out of hand and there was a fight she would be back to square one, with one upstairs and one downstairs. As it was, Ghilly now came into the bedroom at night but still preferred to sleep on the chaise longue, rather than sharing the bed.

Things were definitely improving and not just with the cats. That morning Monica had taken great delight in ringing Sunday 8th March on the kitchen calendar. *Trevor Home* she wrote, and drew a little smiley face next to it. It would be his very last night as John Brown, then he would be home for a rest and they could spend time together. He could meet Ghilly and they would be a family again. Theodosia adored Trevor and would be in seventh heaven when he arrived, just as Monica herself would. Even after all those years together, she still got a thrill when she saw him after time apart.

Around 2 a.m. on Monday 9th Monica finally heard the sound she had been waiting for, Trevor's car pulling onto the drive. She put the book she had been trying to read down, put on her robe and left the sleepy bewildered cats yawning and blinking. As she reached the bottom of the stairs Trevor was just bundling in through the front door, his arms laden down with bags and a huge bouquet of crimson roses.

"Mon!" he said, dropping everything to the floor except for the flowers, which he now held out in front of him, "Mon! I've missed you. Come here."

They stood in the cold hall, hugging one another, the roses squashed between them. Monica soaked up the smell and feel of her husband. It had been such a long time.

"Well," she said after a few moments, "was it a wonderful last night?"

"The best, Mon. They were such a wonderful, generous cast. God, we felt like a family by the end of it. I'll miss them. I'll miss the play. Wonderful, wonderful, people."

"Come on, let's grab a drink and you can tell me about it. Unless you're too tired?"

"No, no I'm on a high. Couldn't sleep if I wanted to……Oh, and who's this?" From the top of the stairs a small dark face peered worriedly down. "This must be my namesake, Ghilly."

As always, Trevor was speaking as though he was still on stage and the young cat was not sure whether to be alarmed or to investigate. As Trevor made towards him, he vanished like a Will-o'- the-wisp back along the landing and into the bedroom.

"Ah well," said Trevor, philosophically. "Let's go and sit down."

There was something very special and cosy about sitting up together, one on either side of the fire, glasses of whisky in their hands, with just the clicks and squeaks of the house for company. Before long Theodosia found them and immediately trotted over to Trevor.

She meowed loudly before jumping up on his lap and fluffing her tail in delight. "What?" said Trevor.

"Are you complaining about the new lodger? Bit of a squirt, I heard. Eh, sweetheart?"

There was another loud, croaking yell from Theodosia which could only be taken as agreement.

"They get on much better now," said Monica. "It was pure hell to start with, like world war three, but they're fine now. Well apart from the occasional spat. Now, tell me about the show….."

As she listened to Trevor recounting various tales from the theatre, she was struck by two things: one, just how much she missed that life, and two just how much she had missed her husband. With his greying hair, straight nose and mischievous grey eyes, he was still a very handsome man - slim, exuberant and funny. The house was a different place when he was home. And tomorrow she would wake up next to him.

Monica slept better than she had in months that night. Just knowing Trevor was there seemed to permeate into her sleep and she relaxed. Both cats were shut out, Theodosia settled in the spare bedroom and after much complaining, Ghilly had taken himself downstairs with a final grumble as he reached the hall.

In the morning Trevor was already up and about when Monica came to. He never was one for wasting the day and she could hear the vibrations from his voice travelling up the stairs. He was probably talking to the cats, getting acquainted with Ghilly. However, when she wandered out onto the landing, both cats were waiting for her, sitting with their legs neatly folded beneath them and looks of expectation on their faces.

"Hello, darlings," she said. "Shall we go and see Daddy. Hasn't he given you your breakfast?" She was as anxious as the cats to go downstairs. She wanted to start making plans for her and Trevor. It would be marvellous to just potter around together.

When she reached the kitchen Ghilly wasn't at all sure he wanted to go in. There was a strange male in his house and he didn't quite know what he should be doing about it.

Trevor was in full flow, a cup of coffee in one hand and his phone in the other. When he saw Monica he waved his cup questioningly at her and mouthed, "Coffee?"

Seeing that he was so busy she gestured that she would make her own. As she did so, she couldn't help listening to what was going on in the one sided conversation.

"Yep, yep, historian, narrator, uh huh. Dance skills? Well, not bad I suppose. How much dancing is there?"

Realizing that this was work, Monica immediately started making faces at him! And shaking her head. This was supposed to be their time.

But Trevor ended the call with, "Yes, I would be interested. Thank you for calling me. Okay, you make the approach and let me know. Thanks. Bye….bye."

He turned to Monica and said, "That was Clara. She's got something I might be interested in."

"Oh, Trevor," said Monica, feeling her irritation rising. "It's nothing soon is it? You've only just come home."

"Well, soonish, Mon. Work is work and this happens to be fabulous work."

"How fabulous?" she asked.

"It's Spamalot. Touring from end of March right through until June. It's a wonderfully funny show and something completely different for me, if you'll excuse the pun. Mon, I want to do it. You know I've always loved the Pythons, and Simon did it last year and he had a whale of a time. He said it was like panto but with class. Clara thinks she can get me in without the big audition process."

Monica looked at her husband's face and knew there would be no dissuading him. She had seen that look so many times; the new project, and the excitement of working on a new character. He wanted to go, it was as simple as that.

She reminded herself how, long ago they had both agreed, that they didn't own each other and as actors, they had to be free to pursue their careers. It was a done deal. But now that one of them wasn't an actor, it was a much more difficult prospect.

Chapter Twenty Five

Outwardly Monica showed no sign of resentment towards her husband for the next two weeks, but inside she was feeling aggrieved and angry. She played at being the happy wife, enjoying their days together, but she knew it was all set to come to an abrupt end and Trevor would be gone again. She would be alone with just the two cats for company and daily visits from Patty.

Theodosia and Ghilly continued to tolerate each other and even shared a bed now and again, but it was obvious that Theodosia was just waiting for him to go back to where he had come from. Until then, it was clear he was here under sufferance.

On Trevor's very last day at home Monica was exceptionally cool with him. It was like an odd compulsion. She knew she should be savouring every last minute, but her anger wouldn't let her. She had to admit to herself that not only was she was going to miss Trevor, she was also a bit envious of him.

She was being a "right cow," in fact. At least that's what she would have said about another cast member acting in that way, but she couldn't help it. Like Theodosia did to Ghilly, she wanted to lash out and hurt him.

Trevor knew how she felt but as always, he chose to ignore it. They had been together for a long time now and there had been many such partings throughout their marriage. He knew the best thing to do was to simply carry on.

"Fancy orange juice, Mon?" he said. "I might as well have something healthy while I can. God knows what I'll get to eat on this tour."

"No, thank you," she said. "What time are you going? I have a lot to do."

"Well, I'll just finish my breakfast and then I'll be out of your hair. I want to be there in plenty of time."

"Good idea."

She wanted to say, *I don't want you to go. I'm bored and lonely. I'll miss you so much.* But instead she went upstairs and found something to do. Ghilly and Theodosia were stretched out on the bed, at opposite ends of course, but they both looked completely peaceful and relaxed. Monica sat down at the dressing table and fiddled pointlessly with her make-up.

About twenty minutes later she heard Trevor in the hall, obviously preparing to leave. He called up to her, "Right, Mon, I'm off! Bye, Theodosia. Bye, Ghilly be good."

Monica went reluctantly to the landing and shouted, "Bye, have a good time. Don't worry about ringing, I know you'll be busy." She should have gone down. She should have gone for one last hug, but she just couldn't. Trevor was going and she couldn't be nice to him. She went back into the bedroom and listened for the car to pull off the drive. She didn't even watch it go.

The promise of spring now seemed an empty one. She was alone again and ahead of her were long trackless days. She looked across at the bed and noticed it now only contained one cat. Ghilly had moved from his patch at the foot and was missing.

Monica wandered apathetically out on the landing. She wasn't in the mood for hide and seek, but a noise from the bathroom immediately caught her attention. It was like a window blind being quickly rotated on its roller. She went to investigate.

Ghilly was sitting next to the toilet, balancing on his haunches, with his front legs reaching upward to the toilet roll holder. He was battering the living daylights out of it. A flurry of shredded tissue flew everywhere as the roll whizzed round and round. He looked like a boxer with some bizarre punch bag. Dummity, dummity, dum, the sound of his paws as they pummelled the unfortunate roll.

The papery, fluffy mess was horrendous but looking at his little serious face so intent on what he was doing, Monica couldn't find it in herself to be angry. The whole scene was just comical. She scooped the kitten up and held him close and kissed his head. She knew animal experts would say she was rewarding bad behaviour, but at that precise moment, Ghilly the clown was just what she needed to lift her spirits.

Still holding him to her, Monica went back into the bedroom and sat on the bed with him. He immediately began to roll about on the duvet, trying to bite his own tail. From the pillow end of the bed

Theodosia opened one eye and watched, like a sleeping dragon. She was keeping a very close eye on developments.

As Monica reached across to give Theodosia a reassuring stroke, a small grey object on the bedside table caught her eye. It was a little shabby teddy bear on a key ring. It was holding a heart shaped sign with "Love You" on it. She had meant to slip it into Trevor's packing last night. It was supposed to say what she couldn't but her moth brain had let her down again, and there it was, just where she had left it.

She had started to grow accustomed to the odd lapses when she just couldn't remember a word or a name, it was just how she was these days, they didn't really matter too much. But this! This time it had really mattered. She could post it on, but that would just seem like an afterthought. Sadly she picked up the bear and slid it into the drawer.

For a long while she sat on the bed staring into space and automatically stroking the kitten at her side. His purrs were the only sound, and as she listened to the silence of the house she realized she really was alone. Going downstairs would only make it seem even more real, so she remained sitting on her bed, waiting for Patty to come and break the stillness.

Over the next few days, Monica began to slip back into the routine she had established for herself before Trevor's homecoming. Having him around had given her a little glimpse of how it might have been but then he was gone. She knew of course, that after a few weeks Trevor would have become restless and wanted to go back to work anyway. She had been exactly the same in the past, whenever she had had enforced time at home, but it would have been so nice to have his company for just a little bit longer.

Retirement wasn't suiting her, but not for one minute would she admit it. It was supposed to be about doing all the things you ever wanted to do, but the truth was, she had been doing exactly what she wanted for years. She had been spoiled, Trevor and her mother had seen to that. Claudette had been fond of saying that there is always an answer, but from where she was, it was hard for Monica to see what that might be. Perhaps she should just get a job, but what was she really qualified to do apart from act?

March had been an indifferent month weather wise, and even the occasional flurry of snow had turned up now and again just to remind everyone that winter had not quite gone. And so it was a relief to Monica to change the calendar and hope for better, brighter things. It would be Easter soon and that was always an uplifting time.

That particular morning the sun was shining, and both cats were sitting on separate window sills 'bird watching'. Now and again Theodosia would let out a curious chattering noise, which Monica always imagined was the cat telling the flying snacks just what she would do to them if she came out there. It sounded so clipped and funny she couldn't help but smile. Contentedly she spread marmalade on her toast and decided this would be a much better month than March.

Trevor had settled into his new role. It was always difficult joining an existing cast but he had managed to charm everyone as usual. Monica had almost forgiven him for going. If only she could find something to do with her time. Last night in bed she had been reading about a woman who had published her first novel at fifty. It sounded relatively straightforward. There seemed to be no training involved, but there was mention of a workshop for new writers.

After finishing her toast Monica made her way upstairs to fetch the magazine. She would find out the name of the workshop and look it up on the internet; she might even enrol. Suddenly the idea of becoming a writer seemed like a fabulous solution. She could write the books at home and then go out and promote them with her acting skills.

As she came back down with the magazine something quite strange happened. It was not at all dramatic, so simple in fact that it was farcical, almost casual. Monica slipped on the bottom stair. She didn't fall, she just slithered down on her back, as though she was merely flowing onto the hall floor. There was no pain, just a sound like a stick of rock snapping.

Feeling oddly calm and still holding the magazine she looked down at her ankle. Her foot was at a ludicrous angle to her leg and appeared to now be boneless and floppy. She sat there for a moment, trying to take in what had just happened. It felt peculiar but tranquil. Leaning forward and pulling up her trouser leg she watched as her ankle seemed to swell in front of her.

It was only when both cats appeared and started to yowl in alarm that she began to panic slightly. What had she done? Ghilly approached cautiously and sniffed her foot, while Theodosia hopped up and down the bottom stairs, head-butting her shoulder.

As she sat there, wondering what to do, the pain began surge along her leg. She knew she would have to move. She would need to get to the phone and call someone. Patty was due in a while, but the pain was mounting rapidly. Grabbing the handrail she tried to drag herself up, but her foot simply wouldn't work. It felt as though she had been sitting with it tucked under her for hours, it was just floppy and useless and any sort of pressure on it made her gasp out loud.

This was serious and fear began to rise in her. As though they sensed it, both cats began cruising back and forth around her. Anxiously Theodosia called out for help in her rusty Siamese voice, a look of alarm in her blue eyes.

The pain was now becoming intense. She closed her eyes and tried to shut it out. Patty would be here soon, she told herself, Patty would be here. All she could do was sit and wait. Even though the hall radiator had automatically clicked on, Monica now felt cold and shaky. She tried to remember the first few lines of Romeo and Juliet, anything to take her mind off the pain, but as always these days, her memory was lacking.

Finally she heard what she had been wishing for, Patty's key in the lock. "Mornin', Mrs P!" she shouted. "Lovely, bright mornin'!"

"Patty, Patty, I'm in the hall. Could you help? I'm stuck," Monica called back, trying not to sound as terrified as she felt.

"Stuck?" said Patty, waddling slowly into the hall. "Oh my God. Whatever have you done?" she said, instinctively trying to pick Monica up.

"No! No ! Patty, no," screamed Monica, clinging desperately to the bannister. "I think I've broken something. Just let me sit here. Please don't pull me. Oh, God."

Sweat was now making its way out on to the surface of Monica's skin, making her feel both cold and clammy at the same time, whilst her head seemed to be puling itself into a tall point.

"Oh, lore," said Patty. " I think you have, an' all. Bloomin' 'eck. Look at size of your foot!"

"Patty, do you think you could you get me a blanket or something? I'm freezing."

"That'll be shock, that will. You can die of that, you can. You just slip into it and bang, you're gone. It's not the injury you see, it's the shock. I'll get you some hot sweet tea."

"No, Patty. Please, just a blanket and ring for an ambulance."

"Right you are, I'll get and phone first," said Patty and then pausing for a moment she said, "You do realize it's April Fools' today, don't you?"

Chapter Twenty Six

Monica looked down at the plaster cast. She didn't know what she hated more about it - the fact that that it existed at all, or that it was such a vivid shade of electric blue. Whatever possessed them to make them in such garish colours these days? she wondered. What was wrong with white? That would have been much more suitable. But here she was plastered in blue and wishing she could take the damned thing off.

It was heavy and ungainly and Monica loathed it. She had already been wearing it for two weeks and another six lay ahead of her. At this point she wasn't quite sure how she would survive. It was so frustrating: no going for walks, no driving, no gardening. Everything had become an enormous task. Just getting up in the morning felt like a major hurdle, bathing with her leg hanging inelegantly out of the bath, so the plaster stayed dry, trying to balance as she dried herself and hobbling about the kitchen trying to make breakfast.

It all took so long. And once she was up there were the clothes! Nothing fitted over her big blue boot and she was forced to 'hang around' in what she could only describe as loose fitting, rehearsal clothes. It really did all combine to make her feel low and frustrated.

If it hadn't been for the cats, she probably would have chosen to stay in bed most mornings rather than face the tedious routine. She had been given a walking frame to help her move around, but it got caught on absolutely everything, and going upstairs with it and both cats in attendance was almost impossible. Plus the fact that it made her feel positively geriatric! When she had been at the hospital, all she had wanted to do was get home, but now the reality had set in; it wasn't just a case of getting home, but coping with being there. Of course it had been lovely when Patty and her son, Paul had fetched her and made sure she had settled in. They couldn't have been kinder, offering all sorts of help and comfort. They really did have hearts of gold, but ultimately she was still alone. Trevor was contracted right through until June and so she just had to endure.

Now, more than ever, she missed her mother; funny, eccentric, spirited Claudette. She would have made this situation so different. At least though, Monica had the cats. Just to have living things in the house with her helped enormously and strangely it was as though they sensed they were needed. They still clearly didn't care for each other's company but they would settle down either side of her as she sat, and neither left her throughout the night. She called them her furry nurses.

She was forced to spend most of her day sitting in the lounge with her leg up on a footstool with two pillows on top for extra height. Patty came in each morning as usual, but now she also shopped and left meals to be warmed up. Monica felt that she had become ancient overnight and needed a home help.

It was astonishing just how much her life had changed in the last year.

Clinging on to one of Trevor's favourite phrases, she told herself that this too would pass, but as far as she was concerned it couldn't pass quickly enough. Television and reading only took up so much of each day for her and she found that she spent a large amount of time simply staring into space, or watching the cats who, now that spring had arrived, were thankfully much more active and entertaining.

Ghilly got bigger every day. He had finally grown into his bat ears but his long back limbs now gave him a strange wheelbarrow look as he trotted about on his dark stick legs.

Theodosia now seemed much more stately compared to Ghilly and it had to be said she had enjoyed stealing the kitten's food a little more than she should have done over the last few months. She now looked every inch the well upholstered dowager.

Without a doubt their antics helped to keep Monica going. Watching them interact was often her sole entertainment apart from the various weird and wonderful conversations she had with Patty, and the nightly phone call from Trevor. The cats were her salvation.

In her head she would often play a little game, imagining what they might be saying to each other. It was ridiculously anthropomorphic of course, but imagination had never been a problem for actors; they couldn't do what they do if they couldn't use their imaginations.

To Monica it seemed that, as Theodosia entered a room, she would sweep regally in and immediately take stock. If Ghilly happened to be on Monica's lap, her look simply said, *Oh, dear. What's that thing doing there? I thought we'd agreed that you were taking it back.* And then she would glide by with an expression of utter disdain on her face. There was no doubt about it, there was something unmistakably aristocratic about the large lilac point. Something that made her seem just a little bit haughty and superior.

Ghilly on the other hand, appeared to have become toughened up by the initial rejection, and now he gave as good as he got. One had to admire his obstinate stand. When Ghilly meowed it was loud and clear, as though he was asserting his rights. Theodosia was not having it all her own way.

Watching their characters grow was a huge comfort to Monica. It was almost like being a child again, escaping to her own make believe world, where she had control over everything, instead of trying to cope with one where she had control over nothing.

On one particular evening, the cats were practicing their own specific type of cat martial arts, or Cat Fu as Monica had christened it. Theodosia was lying on her back on the sofa but keeping the youngster at bay by jabbing at him expertly with one powerful front paw. The inexperienced Ghilly sniped and swiped wildly at any opening he could find. Eventually boring of the game, Theodosia jumped down from the sofa and tried to wander off. Ghilly followed in hot pursuit, nipping at her back legs.

Irritably Theodosia turned, *"You really are a tiresome child,"* she said, or rather Monica said. There was something so irresistible about the situation that meant she simply had to add a voice. As a child she had loved *Animal Magic* and *Tales of the River Bank*; all those creatures and their particular funny ways of speaking, and so this little game of hers seemed to come with total ease. She would be their voices.

"Come back here and fight, ya great Booly," replied Ghilly, in what to Monica's surprise turned out to be a broad Scottish accent.

Whether it was the fact he had come from a Scottish breeder or just something about his slightly truculent air that suggested this, she didn't know, but it was obvious to Monica that this was how he spoke. Scottish and plucky.

"That's it! You run away, hen!" he continued, planting his feet defiantly on the hearth rug. *"You know I've the better of you!"*

"Hmmmph," said Theodosia's imperious, feisty voice. *"You are lucky I am in a good mood, Scotty, or you would be toast."*

"Oh, look at me!" said Ghilly, throwing himself dramatically down on his back and rolling over. *"Look how scared I am of you. Please don't hurt me, Princess Purple Face."*

The words came flowing out of Monica's mouth, each of the two characters having their own facial expressions and distinctive voices. She slipped easily between the two.

"Take yourself away, William Wallace, before I bite you again. Don't try my patience," said Theodosia as she made her way calmly toward the kitchen. *"I'm going for a bite to eat now,"* she said, glancing over her shoulder at him. *"And I don't expect you to follow me, irritant!"*

"Got to keep your strength up, eh?" said Ghilly, watching her go. *"Don't let me stop you. There's an awful lot of you to feed!"*

"I shall ignore that last remark," said Theodosia, sarcastically. *"Simply because I know that you wouldn't dare come here and say it to my face."* With a final dismissive flick of her tail she made her exit while Ghilly settled down to smooth his slightly ruffled fur. To Monica it seemed he was mumbling under his breath as he cleaned, *"Wouldn't say it to your face, wouldn't I? Well, we'll see about that, Princess Poppet Paws. You just wait till you come back in here, biscuit breath. I can wait. You won't see me coming. I'll be like a wee seal point Ninja."*

Laughing to herself, Monica sat back in her chair. She hadn't laughed out loud for so long. It was almost like playing with dolls, but they were alive and moved on their own. It was fun. For a moment she had been acting again and it felt good. But just as she felt her heart lighten, a shadow fell across it. Was this really fun? Or was she going a little ga ga? First her memory loss, and now this? But she hadn't imagined that the cats were actually speaking to her, had she? She knew it was just her, playing. Even so, something dark hung over her for the rest of the evening. Could it really be that she was beginning to lose her mind?

Chapter Twenty Seven

The next day Monica didn't play "The Cat Game." It worried her that she had slipped into it so easily. Her little bit of fun didn't seem so innocent any more. She couldn't make the dark thoughts go away. Talking to yourself was one thing, but being two separate personalities?

As she sat brooding in the lounge, Patty's cow like lowing came to her from the kitchen. She often had a song of the day, or even the week and this time it seemed more appropriate than usual. She had chosen to tunelessly sing the chorus to Cigarettes and Whisky and Wild, Wild Women over and over again, with a particular emphasis on the line, They'll drive you cra-zee, they'll drive you in-sane.'

The more Monica tried to shut it out, the more it resonated in her head. 'They'll drive you crazy, they'll drive you insane.' Normally when Patty decided to have a musical morning, Monica would take herself away into Trevor's office or upstairs but now there was no escape. She was trapped and the tune went on and on.

"Patty," she shouted, hoping to break the cycle. "How's the family?" Even this was preferable to the song torture.

"Not so bad, thanks. Mr P all right in his play, is he?" she said, briefly popping her head round the door.

Monica nodded. Clearly this was not going anywhere and the song was in danger of returning.

"Anything in the paper today? "Monica tried.

"Oh, now't much. The usual rubbish, you know? Young women showing more flesh than you and I have ever had, politicians blaming one another, and famous folk on their holidays."

Having closed that avenue down, Patty went back to her cleaning and back to her singing.

In a desperate attempt to ease her anxiety Monica said, "Patty, do you ever imagine what your cat would say if he could speak?"

Even as she asked the question she regretted it, and the look on Patty's round moon face said it all. "If me cat could speak?" she said, incredulously. "Well, I'd either teck him on a world tour and buy myself a nice house from the profits, either that or I'd sign meself into the local loony bin. What a question, Mrs P. All this sitting about is doing you no good at all, you know? You'll be goin' doolally."

Of course Patty was entirely the wrong person to ask, but Monica had very few options. Patty's response had only served to confirm what she already feared: she was losing her mind.

For the rest of the day Monica desperately tried to keep her brain occupied. She watched as much television as she could stand. She toyed with the idea of watching a DVD, but getting up to put the thing in was a major exercise and once she got down to the player, she wasn't sure she could get back up again. In the end she simply dozed with both cats curled up on her lap, occasionally shifting position and soothing her to sleep. She felt like the old woman in Yeats' poem, "Old and grey and full of sleep and nodding by the fire." At least she could remember the words. That was something, even if they did depress her.

As she ate her lunchtime sandwich, which had been carefully cling wrapped by Patty and placed where she could reach it, Theodosia and Ghilly both decided it would be nice to share. A dark brown paw slipped up over the edge of the plate and tried to hook into the bread. Monica moved her plate higher. Theodosia got to her feet and began to sniff up at the sandwich, causing Monica to lift it even higher until she looked like a waiter about to serve a rather luscious main course with an extravagant flourish.

This had now become normal. She ate all her lunches like this, with one hand in the air, taking small pieces and transferring them quickly to her mouth. She knew that she should have been firmer with them, but they were so persistent. Pushing them from her lap and saying no seemed to have no effect at all and both of them would instantly jump back up with aggrieved expressions on their faces.

For her evening meal, which she liked to eat at the table, she had to start early in order to make sure that both of them were out of the room. Cat wrangling was not easy at the best of times, but with only one good leg, it was extremely complicated. It really was a silly state of affairs and yet she couldn't imagine her life without the two of them. These long, dark days would have seemed even longer and darker without the Siamese.

The cats still weren't the best of friends, that was clear from their body language, but at least most of the hissing had stopped. Monica dreaded taking Ghilly for his 'little boy's operation' as Patty called it. She felt sure that Theodosia would think he was going for good and be outraged when he came back, smelling slightly medicinal but otherwise the same.

For the time being, at least, it wasn't an issue. Monica couldn't drive so there would be no vet trips just yet. Finishing her sandwich, she carefully placed the cling film back over the plate to prevent crumb snuffleage and settled back into the chair.

What was she going to do when all this was over? There was no normal to return to. Before the accident her life had been in flux and it would continue to be so for as far as she could see. She was an actress that couldn't act any more. She was too old to realistically start a whole new career. Where did that leave her?

If only Claudette had been there to make her see the possibilities. Claudette could cut through all Monica's dramas with just a few words. Like the time that, having failed another audition, Monica had tearfully declared she was a terrible actress and was going to give up. Claudette had calmly carried on with her ironing and then said, "Well, if that is your decision, Choupette I will help you look for another job, in an office perhaps. It would be nice for you to have a routine, no? Every day you go at the same time, you come back at the same time, very tranquil."

Realizing that her mother was not going to hysterically beg her to reconsider, within seconds Monica had stopped crying and was passionately explaining how she could never work in an office, that it would be just too dull, and how she belonged on the stage. Claudette had simply finished folding some towels and said, "Bon."

The oddest thing about this little memory was, that it had now been some time since she had thought of her mother. Guilt stabbed at her: this was her mother, her beautiful, eccentric mother. Surely she should never be able to forget her, not even for a moment.

Monica's eyes had begun to sting with emotion and automatically she reached out to touch the cats. Theodosia, who was cleaning herself, began to clean Monica too, her sandpaper tongue flicking over the back of Monica's hand until it's roughness caused her pain. She took her hand away and wept.

When Monica's tears had stopped, she sat tired and runny nosed in her chair, hating the plaster cast, hating her moth brain and hating Trevor for being so far away.

Both cats were now sitting in front of the fire. Theodosia was still washing herself and Ghilly was watching. As the lilac point methodically cleaned her fur, she carefully lifted a leg and went right to the very tip of her toes to make sure that she was immaculate. Monica smiled and thought how self-satisfied she looked.

By contrast Ghilly looked very unimpressed.

"Look at her, Her Majesty the Preen. She really thinks she's the icing on the cake, doesn't she, eh?"

Glancing up, Theodosia said, "*Good grooming is an essential part of being a cat. You would do well to remember that and give your fur a lick over once in a while. There could be anything living in there!*"

"*Oh, you really think you're something, don't you? Look at me, I'm so stunning,*" said Ghilly, prancing sideways towards her.

On cue, Ghilly turned to look at Monica.

"*She thinks she's stunning,*" he said. "*The only way she'd stun anyone is if she were to fall on them. Aye, that would stun you, right enough.*"

"*Oh, ha ha. Very funny, bagpipe boy. I'll have you know, all heads turn when I enter a room,*" countered Theodosia.

"*Is that so? Well, if you don't mind me saying so, hen. I think you might be getting mixed up with heads and stomachs there.*"

Ridiculously, Monica found herself laughing, albeit in a slightly snuffly, teary way, but she was laughing. She had actually made herself laugh.

So what if she was going slightly mad? It seemed to be the only pleasure she had, trapped in his house all alone, like this. Why not give into it as long as she knew it wasn't real, as long as she could differentiate between make believe and reality? What was the problem and what did she really care about Patty's opinion? This was a creative thing, Patty would never understand that. She had the imagination of a carpet slipper.

Logically of course, she could explain it. She knew it was just observation and pre-empting what they were about to do. She had been trained to do it and it felt so good to be using her skills again; what harm could it really do? The truth was, crazy or not, she didn't want to stop.

Chapter Twenty Eight

And so Monica's bleak little world began to be a little more bearable. She had settled into an odd routine, but it suited her. Each morning she would have Patty's company, which she made the most of - even Patty's tales of peculiar family members seemed of interest now that she was trapped at home and away from the normality of the outside world.

Every day she did her best to engage her cleaner in some sort of conversation, even if sometimes it was just about the weather. But now and again there were the inevitable Patty gems, like the tale of her Aunt Eunice who had answered a lonely hearts advert in the paper and ended up meeting a transvestite from Southport. "He had better dress sense than our Eunice, apparently", chortled Patty. "Shame really, these days nobody would have minded."

On the whole, Monica tried to remain patient, knowing that one day the cast would be removed and she could get on with her life. Until then, she just had to make the best of it. At least now she was beginning to find ways of coping and part of that was the cat game, her own secret pleasure. Once Patty had gone for the day, Monica was free to imagine anything she wanted, just like being a child again, playing in a dolls' house with her living toys. The pleasure she derived from imagining the various scenarios for the two cats was immense.

Mostly she didn't have to think too much about it, ideas simply presented themselves. Only the day before, Ghilly had arrived in the lounge dragging one of her bras behind him. He had obviously been hunting in the linen basket and claimed it as a prize.

He proudly came in with it trailing down from his mouth along the floor under his belly and straggling out behind him. Taking care not to catch his back legs in it, he placed it on the floor for her and Theodosia to admire.

"Get a load o' this! Some sort of weird bag thing. It's great for dragging round and about though. Do yer want a go?"

"I'll pass, thank you," said Theodosia scornfully, looking up from her self-administered manicure.

"Ah, you don't know what you're missing, Princess Poison. You've no joy in you, that's your problem. Always titivating yourself up and never having any fun! A good run round with a wee furry mouse would do you the world of good, if you ask me."

"Well, I didn't ask you, did I? What would be the point of asking you anything? You have the intellect of a retarded gnat."

"Aye, aye, if you say so, but thinking about it, you probably can't run around now, can you?"

"Why not? What do you mean by that, Eric Liddel?"

"Well, you must know, you're a bit, what shall I say? Broad in the beam?"

"What!" hissed Theodosia, threateningly. *"I'll show you who can't run."* And the two of them shot out of the room and up the stairs, Ghilly pausing only to grab his prized bra.

Monica winced as they crashed about on the floor above. From some of the noises she could tell what was going on, but others completely baffled her.

Since she had been immobile, this was another of the problems she had encountered. Noises off, she called it. The sudden alarming crash or rumbling noise coming from another room. Now, she found it best to ignore them. In the beginning she had laboriously made her way to the room where the fracas was taking place, only to be met by the liquid blue gazes of the two most innocent cats in the world.

"Nothing to see here!"

"Nothing amiss at all."

"We're just sitting."

Later she would sometimes find out what they had been up to, but on the whole it was better that she didn't know.

She had asked Patty to pack away as many ornaments as possible. She was clumsy with her walking frame and the cats frequently tore through the house like a storm. The cleaner was only too pleased to oblige. "Muck 'arbourers," she said as she boxed things up. "You wouldn't be so keen on all these if you had to dust them," she added for good measure.

So the house was a little more sparse but at least the ominous crashes didn't worry Monica half as much. She couldn't chase after them so the cats had to be free to do as they liked. She could almost hear Claudette laughing at her and reminding her to "embrace the chaos." She liked to think that her eccentric mother would have approved of her voice game.

Today was a little slow on the cat play front. Theodosia was dozing next to the radiator and Ghilly was sitting on the window ledge watching two blackbirds, who were doing a mating madrigal on the lawn. Suddenly he dropped down from the sill, stretched and prowled over to the sleeping lilac point.

Without warning he plonked himself down right on top of her. Instantly Theodosia woke and hissed loudly, lashing out with a front paw, delivering a swift blow to Ghilly's nose.

"I was asleep!" she spat furiously. *"What do you want?"*

"A wee bit of room would be nice, Your Enormity. I quite fancied a sleep myself. Budge over."

Theodosia licked herself indignantly, got to her feet and vacated the bed.

"Hmmmph," she said. *"I will not be sharing a bed with you, thank you very much."*

She stretched, then immediately jumped onto the sofa and grabbing a cushion with her front paws proceeded to kick it viciously with her back ones. Pausing, she looked across at Ghilly, *"This is your face, Jockstrap,"* she said.

Large threads were now standing proud on the cushion and Monica felt it was time she intervened. "Theodosia!" she said. "Stop that, you'll have it in holes."

"But I'm doing his FACE!" the cat replied, aggrieved. *"He needs to be told."*

When Monica was acting out these little plays, it was almost as though the characters she had invented took over. At times she wasn't even sure what they would say next and sometimes what they did say was so unexpected that it made her laugh out loud.

Their personalities had grown in her mind and now had such depth that she felt she knew them. Perfect, superior Theodosia with her edge of haughty spite; and pugnacious, truculent Ghilly, determined to stand his ground whatever put downs came his way. Monica delighted in their interplay and revelled in their arguments.

But it wasn't all out war. Sometimes Theodosia would lie in her bed with the most beatific expression on her face, as if she was dreaming of some happy land full of fish and shiny bags of treats, but Monica suspected something more sinister than that...... more along the lines of,

"Mother, come quickly the kitten has fallen into the shredder!" or *"Oh how tragic, Ghilly seems to have been trapped in the fridge all night!"* There was no doubt in Monica's mind that Theodosia would

have wished Ghilly away in a heartbeat, and her idea of the two cats bonding and being perfect company for each other was a foolish one.

They would on occasion curl up together, usually on very chilly spring evenings, but even then Theodosia always insisted that it was purely for warmth and that she would need a very good clean afterwards to get the smell off her fur.

Patty loved them both, but it was obvious that she had a particular soft spot for her old friend Theodosia, and it was almost as if Ghilly sensed it. He was never nasty to Patty but he did keep a very close eye on her as she went about her business each day.

Today, shortly after Patty's arrival, it was clear that something had really upset him. He had followed Patty from room to room, keeping up a constant conversation, punctuated with little chirrups.

"What's up with 'is Lordship, this morning?" enquired Patty. "He's certainly got a lot to say for 'imself."

"Who knows, Patty. Something is not to his liking and he's reading you the riot act," laughed Monica, watching the indignant sway of Ghilly's hind quarters as he trailed after the hapless cleaner.

"By 'eck, he's worse than a shop steward," commented Patty.

That was it! That was exactly what Ghilly reminded Monica of, a truculent trades unionist, asserting his rights. She imagined him berating Patty:

"*Now see here, this won't do at all. According to article seven, paragraph four: No cat, Siamese or otherwise should be disturbed by a the use of a vacuum cleaner in their immediate vicinity. That is the situation and by continuing to use this implement you are in fact in breach of our rights, as cats! And furthermore, I think we would be quite within those rights to demand action if this is not rectified by the management straight away.*"

Monica began to laugh. A huge smile spread across her face as she thought about Ghilly's tirade to Patty.

"What's up wi' you!" said Patty, looking up. "Sitting there with a big daft smile on yer face? What's tickled your fancy?"

Not for one moment did Monica have consider trying to explain the joke, it had to remain her secret entertainment, her happy little world of insanity, ironically invented to keep her sane.

Chapter Twenty Nine

It was a particularly wet and blustery April afternoon, as though spring had decided that everywhere would benefit from a good wash and brush up before summer arrived. The rain bounced down in large heavy drops and the wind whipped it into sheets of pale mist sweeping across the front of The Stonehouse.

Monica was glad that she was safely inside, there were advantages to being housebound now and again, and this was one of them. She was sitting in her cosy kitchen attempting to do a rather complicated jigsaw of a Venetian scene. It came out most afternoons but between her own impatience and the cats' insistence on supervising, it had never got further than a piece of gondola and a strip of milky green water.

Theodosia was curled up in her favourite chair near the radiator and Ghilly was walking amongst the jigsaw pieces knocking them around in the lid with his quick brown paws. *"Look here, I've found a wee bit of sky,"* he said.

"I'm doing the Grand Canal first, Ghilly," Monica replied.

"That's a mistake, if you don't mind me saying? You should always start on the sky. It's a well-known fact, sky first. Everything else follows."

"Is it?"

"Oh, aye. Everyone knows that....."

Just then the weather outside became even more violent. The wind rushed at the house with full force, splattering rain hysterically against the windows. The intensity of it was so strong that the back door suddenly blew open and then creaked to a halt.

Trevor had been nagging her for ages to get a new door but she had been stubborn. She liked her stable door, she had told him, it was in keeping with the house. But at that very moment she regretted her decision. The old door had swung back on its hinges and there was now a gap wide enough for a cat to escape through.

Making a grab for her walking frame, Monica desperately tried to stand. If the cats got out into the garden she would have no chance of catching them, she had to get to the door. But before she even managed to haul herself upright, Ghilly had jumped down and was racing towards the gap.

Theodosia, who had never shown the slightest inclination to go outside, merely glanced up from her kitchen chair, as though she was slightly annoyed by the draught, but Ghilly was already sniffing at the opening. Monica made her way over to him as quickly as she was able, but he had already set paw outside.

Abruptly he shot vertically up with his back fur raised and tail bushed. It was so fast that Monica almost didn't see him move. Somehow he had managed to step out of the door, jump straight up in the air, turn round and skitter back into the kitchen. The whole movement was over in seconds.

With enormous round eyes, and bushed tail, Ghilly looked up accusingly at her.

"What in the name of…., all the, what was that?

He began shaking his back feet and licking frantically at his front ones.

In reply a laconic voice came from the kitchen chair, *"That, Scotland the Brave, is rain."*

"Whaat? Well, I can't say a care for that one little bit. What does it do?"

"It makes one wet, haggis breath. If you are stupid enough to go out in it, that is. Personally I keep well away."

"Well nobody mentioned this to me. Does it ever come in here at all?"

"No, it's an outside thing, shortbread brain!"

"Oh, please pardon my ignorance, Your Vastness."

"Well honestly, you make such a fuss. It's just a bit of wet stuff, not sulphuric acid."

"Aaaah, Theodosia," said Monica, shutting the door." Don't be so hard on him, he's just a kitten. He hasn't experienced it before."

"Oh, please don't humour him, Mother. Come over here and see me. I'd like a stroke."

"I'd like you to have a stroke as well," mumbled Ghilly, licking his rain tainted fur indignantly.

"What!" roared Theodosia. *"Zip it, Rob Roy. Don't make me get off this chair."*

"Now, now," soothed Monica. "Let's just forget about the rain and go back to where we were, shall we?"

As she resumed her seat at the kitchen table, she felt quite pleased with herself, until it occurred to her that what she had actually done, was succeeded in breaking up an imaginary argument. Whether it was in her head or not, it had the required effect. Theodosia settled back down in her chair with her tail tucked neatly over her nose and Ghilly resumed his post as jigsaw assistant-in-chief.

For the rest of the afternoon, all was peaceful. Even the weather decided to calm itself a little. The nights were really drawing out now and although it had been such a stormy day, there was a last little bit of golden sunshine breaking through the cobalt coloured clouds, and Monica felt at peace.

She had now learned how to bathe successfully whilst accommodating her plaster and so, after completing a major part of the Doges Palace and finishing a huge mug of coffee, she decided to treat herself to a long soak.

The easiest way by far to get upstairs, was to go up backwards and on her bottom; she had become quite adept at it now. Ghilly would usually accompany her, swiftly flitting up ahead of her and then gambolling back down to check her progress.

She kept a plastic carrier bag in the bathroom to cover her plaster and a stick-on inflatable pillow, which she fixed to the edge of the bath to rest her leg on, while it stuck out at a ludicrous angle. Inelegant didn't begin to cover it, but it was effective and it meant she could lose herself in the warmth of the water for a while, even if it was with one cold leg hanging over the side of the bath.

Normally Ghilly would sit on the toilet lid, watching her from a safe distance. It obviously fascinated him that she immersed herself in water, but he didn't want to investigate too closely. Today he hadn't followed her, but she had left a "cat gap" in the bathroom door, just in case.

When the bath was full of soothing perfumed water, she carefully lowered herself in and released a huge sigh of satisfaction. This was the closest thing to relief that she had experienced since breaking her ankle, a slight weightlessness and the feel of the water lapping against her body. How much she had taken for granted before her accident!

She lay back, taking care to make sure that her leg was safely out of the water and relaxed. Steam rose up in front of her face and she felt totally cocooned in comfort. She rested her head back and let out a huge happy sigh. For a few moments she was totally content.

And then, she started to hear noises coming from the hall. Just little noises, strange rustling sounds and muffled squeaks. It couldn't be anything too bad. Noises off usually began with an almighty crash. This was altogether different, this was……..stealthy.

She lay perfectly still and listened. For a moment it was totally quiet. "Ghilly?" she called. "Ghilly, what are you doing?"

Nothing, not a sound. She tried again. "Ghilly! Come up here. I want to see you."

She waited for the patter of his feet on the stairs, but nothing happened.

Then came another odd sound, a kind of slithering noise followed by a very angry yowl from Theodosia.

Monica pulled herself upright in the bath and listened. Once again, silence. She strained to listen and just faintly she heard a sound like a blanket being folded.

It couldn't be that bad could it? Another yowl reached her from the hall and she knew she had no choice. She struggled out of her lovely warm bath, balanced herself against the wash basin and pulled on her robe. Still dripping, she hopped to the top of the stairs and looked down.

There on the hall floor was the rug which had previously been hanging on the first landing wall. It was a beautiful hand woven masterpiece in glorious colours. Monica liked to call it her flying carpet, and now it had somehow managed to fly down the stairs and land in a heap.

As she laboriously bumped downstairs on her bottom, the rug erupted and she could tell that both of the cats were rumbling about underneath it.

"Stop it, you two! Get out of there."

Ghilly's head appeared and then swiftly ducked back inside, followed by more tunnelling and shuffling, deep in the folds of the rug.

"Ghilly!" she shouted.

This time he came out, but immediately started jabbing at a lump in the rug, which Monica took to be Theodosia.

"Just having a wee game of poky paw," he said, gazing up at her with huge innocent eyes.

By now Monica was over half way down, leaving a trail of drips behind her.

"Get out of there! That's my beautiful rug."

"Oh, I've been meaning to ask you about that. Why was it on the wall, if it's a rug?"

"I liked it there! Now stop it."

"I'm just getting The Goblin Queen, here," he said, pouncing on the rug with both front paws as though he was catching a mouse.

Theodosia let out an irritable squeak and shot out from the folds, shaking herself.

"Get off me, Sporran Boy!" she said, giving him a poisonous look.

"No more!" said Monica, clapping her hands. Both cats looked totally amazed that she wanted them to stop and Monica could almost hear them thinking. "They are so peculiar, these humans. They hang rugs on the wall instead of putting them on the floor and don't understand even the basic rules of poky paw."

Smiling to herself, Monica bumped down the last few remaining stairs and did her best to retrieve the flown carpet.

Chapter Thirty

"Come here Ghilly and listen to this," said Monica holding up a news cutting. "It's from Daddy and there's a note too." Ghilly's dark, velvety face looked in her direction and registered just the slightest flicker of interest. He had found himself a nice cosy spot lying along the top of the radiator in the kitchen. Patty often dried her cloths there and they made excellent cushions.

"*Wha-sat*?" he said, swiping a paw over his ear and letting it ping up again. "*What ya say*?"

"Well, if you came in here you'd know, wouldn't you? Come on, Ghilly I want to read this to both of you."

Theodosia had already established herself on Monica's lap and was purring robustly.

"*Okay, I'll be there in a tick,*" said Ghilly, "*although it may take a wee while to circumnavigate Queen Theodosia The Great when I get to your lap. Are you sure I couldn't just listen from here?*"

"Ghilly!"

"*Ah, okay, okay, I'm on my way. Keep your wig on.*"

The seal point hopped casually down and sauntered towards Monica, right on cue.

"*So, what are you goin' on about*?" he said, settling himself on the rug. "*Okay if I stay here? Your lap appears to be full, just now.*"

"Well it's your choice, Ghilly. Now, listen to this:

Trevor Pinto's sly interpretation of the historian/narrator was as entertaining as it was thought provoking and definitely in the in Python tradition. A safe pair of hands to hold the show together and keep it moving for the audience. And then it talks about the others in it. Isn't that wonderful?"

"*It's marvellous, Mother,*" said Theodosia, letting out a long, low purr.

"*Do you think so?*" said Ghilly.

"Oh, Ghilly, don't be so negative. He might not have got a mention at all. They singled him out. And wait for this, he says he will be popping in on his way south and we can all spend a few days together."

"*Well, if you say so, but it'll be good to see him.*"

"*Oh, will it?*" said Theodosia. "*You were terrified of him last time he was here, running around screaming that we had an intruder.*"

"*Just a small mistake on my part. There's no need for you to bring that up.*"

"Well, you'll know this time won't you, Ghilly? And we can have a lovely time, all together," said Monica, happily.

For the next few days Monica was in a cloud of happiness and anticipation. Like a child waiting for a birthday to come she planned and imagined.

She had instructed Patty to use the best bedding. She laid out new potpourri in every room and freshly cut spring flowers sat proudly at each window. Her three precious 'Trevor days' were planned out in detail.

What had pleased her most was the discovery that a dark sock stretched over her plaster, teamed with a suitably long skirt, made her hideous blue boot almost disappear. They could dine out, go where they pleased and she wouldn't feel that she was being stared at.

It would all be very different when Trevor arrived. The house would be full of laughter and fun again and he would have someone to talk to other than Patty and the cats.......oh yes, the cats. She decided that she wouldn't tell Trevor about the cat game although she really wasn't sure what was stopping her. But whatever the reason, it felt at that precise moment like it should remain her secret.

On the evening before he was due home, Monica received a phone call from a very sheepish Trevor.

"Mon, the thing is, they've added another couple of nights to the run. I mean it's marvellous, for us, but."

"But you won't be coming home," said Monica, finishing his sentence. "Oh, Trevor. I've been looking forward to it. Have you any idea what my life is like, stuck here day after day?"

"I know, I know, darling. If I could get back I would, you know that. It's just one of those things. You've got Patty and the cats. Why don't you call some of our friends for a chat."

"Oh yes, good idea, except they are all acting. It's what they do! What could I possibly have to talk about. I don't bloody well act any more, remember?"

"Mon, come on. I know it's hard but the plaster will be off soon and then.."

"And then what? All my troubles will be over, and I'll magically get a life? Trevor, I'm going now. I need to get over this. I'll call you when I feel better. Goodbye."

As she pressed End Call, Monica knew she had acted appallingly. She was just so disappointed. She knew Trevor had no choice but she wanted him to suffer. It wasn't fair, but it was how she felt.

For a long while she just sat and stared into space. She wasn't even thinking of anything, just her own sadness. It felt as though she was slipping down into the darkness. It had never occurred to her for one minute that Trevor wouldn't come home. She felt so stupid. She had been in the business long enough to know how quickly plans can change, but this time she couldn't shrug it off. This had been her lifeline and without it she felt adrift on a black sea.

Unchecked tears coursed down her face and dripped from her chin. Since Claudette had gone, her emotions seemed so much closer to the surface, raw and visceral and likely to overflow. Knowing that she would not be able to stem the flood, Monica ran the heel of her hand along her wet jawline and wiped it on her sweater.

After an hour of silent tears, Monica dragged herself to her feet and made her laborious way upstairs to bed.

In the morning, the spring sunshine shone into her bedroom and two sleepy cats yawned and gently head-butted her into wakefulness.

"Hello, darlings," she said, genuinely pleased by their affection. "How are you this morning?" Ghilly climbed up onto her chest, ran his face along her cheek and looked intently at her with his vivid sapphire eyes. Sometimes she didn't need to invent voices for them, it was obvious what was needed - breakfast.

Over the next few days Monica continued to feel bereaved. Trevor would be on his way to the next venue now, without even being able to pop in, and it hurt. Patty had been her usual imperturbable self when Monica had told her the news about Trevor and simply commented, "Aye well, absence makes the heart grow fonder, I suppose. What do you want in your sandwiches, dinner time?"

In the face of such indifference Monica was left to pick up the pieces but like the Venetian jigsaw scene, some of the pieces were just a little bit ragged at the edges.

One afternoon when television had once again driven her into a state of suffused irritation, she threw down the remote control and looked about the room. Everything was peaceful. Both cats had found gloriously comfortable positions to sleep in and Monica felt totally alone.

Just as she was wondering what on earth she could do to pass the time, Ghilly stirred. Immediately alert he dropped down from his sunny window ledge and came over to her, chatting and chirruping as he came. Lovingly he rubbed around her legs, taking special care to leave his mark on Monica's plaster.

"Hello, you," she said, leaning forward to stroke him. "Have you had a good sleep? Come and talk to me for a while, I'm so bored."

Ghilly leapt up onto her lap and trampled vigorously on her knees.

"What you need," he said, *"is a hobby. Something you can really get stuck into, no jigsaws and alike, something...... I don't know, creative maybes."*

"Oh, Ghilly, believe me, before you came, I tried a few things out for size: book club, a choir, gardening. Nothing much seemed to fit."

"How about something you can do sitting down, just till your leg gets better? You know, like painting? Something like that?"

"Well, I was thinking of taking up writing at one point, maybe I should. What do you think? Perhaps I could do plays? I know about staging, directing. All you need is a good idea."

"Why not? You know, I thought I might have a wee go at writing a story myself."

"Really, Ghilly, did you? What would it be about?"

"Most probably a handsome young Seal Point cat and his fight with the evil Queen Clawrine. What do you think?

"I think you're an idiot, that's what I think," said Theodosia, opening her eyes fully and fixing him with a disdainful glare.

"Oh, do you now. Well I think you are a big lazy old walrus of a cat that does nothing but lie about cleaning her mangy old fur all day. You know what they say, you can't polish a……"

"Ghilly!" shouted Monica. "That will do."

"Well, it's her, always yapping on at me about something. I know she is the senior cat here, but she really makes the most of it."

"Yes, I AM senior cat, Rob Roy, and don't you forget it!"

"You see, there! She never calls me by my own name, it's always something sarcastic."

"Look, Jockstrap I didn't ask for your company, it was foisted upon me. Don't expect me to be happy about it, because I won't be! I was quite happy here with Mother and Patty and then you came along, with your noise and your smells!"

"Noise and smells? You know you snore, don't you? Rumble pig skin! You're like a dinosaur with the belly ache when you get going. And smells, well, I'm too much of a gent to comment, but I have had the misfortune to follow you on the litter tray a few times, if you get my drift?"

"I DO NOT SNORE AND I DO NOT SMELL. How dare you even suggest it!" bellowed Theodosia.

Oddly, at this point, Ghilly wandered up and hit the top of Theodosia's head with a resounding thunk. The timing couldn't have been more perfect.

"Aw, put a sock in it, Queen of The Pig People. I've had enough of you today," he said.

Theodosia let out an short irritated meow and said, *"Mother! Are you going to allow him to assault me?"*

"Look," said Monica, "I think we should all calm down a little, don't you?"

In the kitchen Patty was standing very still. She had popped back to bring Monica a "Learn To Crochet" magazine, with a ball of wool and a hook free inside. At first she had thought there were visitors arguing in the house, but now she realized to her horror, that although she could hear three distinct voices, they were all coming from Monica.

Chapter Thirty One

Carefully, Patty pushed open the lounge door. For a second, Monica looked surprised, before turning her expression into one of affected joy.

"Patty, hello. How lovely. I wasn't expecting you to pop in," she said.

"What you doin'?" said Patty, suspiciously.

"Nothing, just talking to the cats, they've been so restless this afternoon."

"I know, I heard. But I mean, what are you DOIN'? You were talking in different voices. Are you feeling right?"

"Oh, yes fine," said Monica, flapping her hand in dismissal, clearly hoping the subject would be dropped. "So, why have you called in anyway, Patty?"

"I bought you this," said Patty, holding up the magazine. "Thought you could learn something useful. There's wool in it and an 'ook."

"Thank you, that's so thoughtful of you. I'll have a look at that later."

Patty slowly put the magazine down on the coffee table. "Mrs P," she said. "You are all right, aren't you?"

"Yes, of course I am."

Patty folded her arms and drew in a long slow breath.

"Well, don't take this the wrong way, but you don't seem right to me, sat there talking to yourself."

"Oh, Patty I was just having fun. You know actors are all a little eccentric."

"Hmmmm, I dare say but there's eccentricity and there's plain barminess. Take my cousin Frank, he were eccentric, thought he were a Viking, even went so far as to give his dog a Viking funeral in his back garden. But the thing is, it turned out he really was descended from Vikings, so it were all right. But this? This is just worrying, sitting here all alone, doing different voices it's, ...unhealthy. You've not been right since Claudette went."

"I'm fine," Monica snapped.

"But since Claudette...."

"I don't want to talk about it, Patty. I said I'm fine."

Monica's voice sounded strained as she tried to end the conversation, but Patty continued.

"Well, the thing is, Mrs P if I've got summat to say, I believe in saying it. You have not been at all yourself, not since the Christmas before last and your poor mother. Giving up your acting, forgetting things, getting odd notions in your head, having fancies about things. And all this joining things. You won't hide from yourself in a club or a choir. And today, well today is the tin lid. And don't say it's nothing because I know otherwise….. I've seen it before."

"I don't know what you mean. You have a very strange view of me, if that is what you really think."

"Oh, really. Well, I saw me granddad go like it. Lovely man he were, always laughing and joking, soft as a brush, and he'd give you his last penny if you needed it. Anyway, he started forgetting things, just like you do, little things at first and then they were happening more and more. Me grandma made excuses for him, but we all knew he weren't right. Then he started the talking, sat by himself in the garden talking away. *Eccentric,* me gran said, *he's not hurting anybody*. And it's true he weren't to begin with, but then one night in bed, me gran felt his hands sliding round her throat and he were trying to kill her as she lay there. That's how eccentric he were!"

"Oh rubbish, Patty. He was obviously a very sick man. This is totally different. There's nothing like that wrong with me," countered Monica, irritably.

"You think so? Well I'm only telling you what happened because this looks very familiar to me and I think you want to watch yourself."

"I'm bored. I was just passing the time. I'm an actress, it's what I do."

"Not any more you're not and not sat here all by yourself doin' it neither. That's just downright peculiar is that. Look, I'm speaking to you as a friend now, I really think you should go and see the doctor. Let me make an appointment for you. I've got the number for the health centre in me bag, I'll find it."

Monica's outrage boiled over. She had had enough of the conversation and enough of Patty's wild accusations. Slowly she pulled herself upright in her chair and prepared to speak. With all the Lady Macbeth venom she could muster, she said, "I have tried to be good natured about this, but it really is too much. How dare you stand there and insult me in my own home. What I do, or don't do is not your concern. You are here to clean, not lecture me and tell tales about your monstrous abnormal family. And as for being friends, I would hardly describe us as that."

Patty visibly flinched and stepped back slightly from the tirade. For a moment she was silent before saying quietly, "Well, if that's how you feel about it, I shall be off. But I'll say this, I was brought up to tell the truth and shame the devil, and that's what I've done. And if it's not to your liking, then I'm sorry, but it had to be said. I'll leave your key."

After one last steady look, Patty turned and left the room. Monica heard her place her key on the kitchen dresser as she went. The back door was firmly closed and Patty was gone. So that really was that. She had lost her cleaner.

For a while Monica sat in her armchair, shaking with an odd mixture of fury and offence, going over the conversation in her mind and wishing she had said more. It really was quite breath taking to be preached to about one's sanity, especially by someone like Patty.

Unable to go for a long walk to rid of herself of the frustration Monica settled on the nearest thing to it, going from room to room with her walking frame. Agitatedly she picked things up and put them down again, not really noticing what she was doing. Her mind and body were working totally separately.

As if they sensed trouble, both cats pretended to be asleep at opposite ends of the sofa. Human anger and shouting was not to their liking. It made them curl up just that little bit more tightly and close their eyes just a little more firmly, to shut out the unpleasantness of people.

Eventually Monica paused and stood in the kitchen. She stared out into the long garden of The Stonehouse and tried to find comfort in natural things. The spring light was beginning to fade, a sharp little breeze shook catkins on the ancient Silver Birch and rattled the trellis on the potting shed. She relaxed her eyes and let it all blur, but to her surprise, far from feeling at peace Monica found that she was still furious over the exchange with Patty, indignant that she could even have mentioned such a thing. Who was she? Just an ignorant woman, full of old wives tales and tall stories. Why should she listen to her? It was ludicrous. Nonetheless she began to feel that part of her anger was not only with Patty.

Slowly making her way back into the lounge in search of the cats, Monica hid behind her self-righteousness. "Well, darlings," she said, "I'm sorry about that, but sometimes people go too far and they have to be told."

Theodosia rose slowly and stretched out along the sofa, knocking Ghilly with her paw as she did so. Normally this would have been a golden opportunity for a pithy comment but for once, Monica didn't immediately spring to put words into their mouths. After her exchange with Patty the cat chats didn't seem quite so funny.

For the rest of the evening Monica brooded. There was no other way to describe the dark mood that overwhelmed her. She ate her evening meal and tried to watch the television but all the time an unease weighed down on her, like a physical pressure in her chest. An undefinable something that had been keeping her company since Patty left.

Finally sitting there in the darkening room, she recognized what it was that was haunting her. It was fear; she was afraid of what was happening to her, afraid of what she might become and afraid that Patty was right. What if she really was becoming a danger to people? What if she hurt Trevor, or the cats? She started to feel heat rising inside her, spreading from her chest to her neck and then finally to her face. She felt engulfed by panic.

Why had she had reacted so badly to what Patty had said if she wasn't afraid? She had been overly defensive, rude and irrational. She would ring her and apologize immediately. But as she started to punch in the number she could almost hear Patty's smug northern tone saying, "Aye well, you know what they say, truth 'urts!"

She put the phone down and, picking it up again, she dialled a different number. After a click the recorded voice at the end of the line said: *Welcome to The Stowe Practice. This surgery is now closed. If* you think you are in need of urgent medical attention, please replace the receiver and dial 999, if not please call back tomorrow. Our opening hours are 8.00.am to 600.pm Monday to Friday. Thank you.

Chapter Thirty Two

As soon as Monica took her seat in the waiting room she knew it was a mistake. She didn't belong here with these people. Actors never went to the doctors, they simply got on with it until something really serious finally stopped them. They went down fighting, they didn't go about silly ailments. But Patty had been adamant. If Monica wanted her to return she had to promise to see a doctor, and so what had been a spur of the moment phone call had turned into action.

She was still inclined to think that it was all a storm in a tea cup, but Patty had been so alarmed by "the voices," it seemed easy to make the promise. A quick trip to the GP and it would all be forgotten. But now she was actually here, she found herself feeling apprehensive.

Patty had loaded her into the taxi that morning with an air of stoic resignation, almost as though she was sending her off to the vet with a very sick animal.

"You'll see, it'll be for the best in the long run. Now take my cousin Wendy, she were like you, wouldn't go anywhere near the doctors but…….. well, no, no, I won't tell you about her. It didn't end well. But the thing is, you couldn't go on as you are. You have to get some help."

Now, Monica looked around the GP's surgery and regretted her decision. There was no one else in the room who seemed to be like her. They were either much older or young mums with children. She felt a complete and utter fraud. She didn't really have anything wrong with her, apart from her ankle of course, and that was mending. But she was here now, she couldn't very well leave, and anyway she had come by taxi so it wasn't as simple as just making a quick exit. And then she would have to face Patty of course. Lugubrious prophet of doom, Patty with her dire warnings of insanity.

Reconciled to her predicament Monica tried to see how things worked, if there was a pattern, so she could see who was next. But as far as she could tell, no one was going in or out of the doctor's consulting room. They were all just sitting.

Some of the older ladies had started up conversations and appeared to be quite enjoying themselves. They didn't seem the least bit worried by the lack of progress. Perhaps they were accustomed to it? They must be professional doctor botherers, Monica decided. This would be the highlight of the week for them, a chance to compare illnesses and procedures. They certainly seemed to know all the medical terms as ectomies and oscopies were bandied about freely.

In the corner a little girl was pushing shiny, coloured beads around a metal frame, while her mother constantly reassured her that she wouldn't be long.

"Going in, in a minute, Anb'. Won't be long now."

Monica pondered the *Anb.* Annabelle, perhaps? It was certainly an odd shortening.

She didn't have to wait long. Seeing the child was becoming agitated the mother snapped, "Ann Boleyn, play quietly. I told you, it won't be long,"

Ann Boleyn! Who would name a child Ann Boleyn? Monica wondered. Perhaps she had five sisters? it was too grisly to think about, but then the mystery was solved. A nurse came out from a side room and called, "Amber Lyn Clarke, would you like to come through please?"

Smiling to herself Monica watched as *Ann Boleyn* and her mother followed the nurse. With that little distraction over, she went back to looking around her for things of interest. By now she was utterly bored and started to read the ancient corner curled posters on the notice board.

AFRAID TO GO HOME?

BLOW THE WHISTLE ON DOMESTIC VIOLENCE.

LIVING WITH CANCER?

TEN THINGS YOU SHOULD KNOW.

BLOOD IN YOUR URINE?

DON'T IGNORE IT

MAKE AN APPOINTMENT WITH YOUR GP

And a rather gruesome one showing someone receiving a bolt of lightning to the head:

MIGRAINE?

DON'T SUFFER IN SILENCE, TALK TO YOUR DOCTOR.

How depressing it must be to be a doctor, she thought, there are so many things that can go wrong with people. You must feel like the whole world is ill, hearing these things day after day.

At last the surgery door slowly opened and an a very old woman with both of her legs completely bandaged, crept painfully out.

"Thank you, Doctor. Thank you for your time. God bless you," she said, and once again Monica felt a pang of guilt. What was she doing here? It would be embarrassing going in there and telling a complete stranger how she felt. Panic started to rise in her and she realized she had forgotten the clever little speech she had made up in her head for the doctor. The one about being a little forgetful, the one about age catching up with her. It had been so light hearted and perfectly pitched but now she couldn't remember a word of it.

"Monica Pinto, please," called a voice from beyond the door. Too late, she was on!

Today Monica was walking with just a crutch. The frame was just too difficult to bring and so she made her way slowly to the consulting room, being avidly watched by her fellow captives who had nothing better to do. No doubt they would have an interesting few minutes imagining how she might have broken it.

Finally, safely inside and with the door shut behind her, she flopped gratefully down in the chair. Sitting at the desk, patiently waiting for her to settle, was a young Asian woman in a brightly coloured headscarf who, to Monica's eyes at least, looked to be no more than seventeen.

"I am Doctor Jawad. What can I do for you today?" she said, confidently. "Is your leg bothering you?" she continued, glancing at the record on her screen.

"Errm no, well, yes of course it is, but I... "

"Okay, but that's not what you are here for. We don't see you very often, Monica so take your time, don't be nervous. How can I help you?"

It was now or never, but Monica had no idea where or how to begin. The glib little speech she had invented had long since flown away with the moths and now all she was left with was a totally blank brain. What did she want to say?

For a moment Monica felt overwhelmed with a sense of such hopelessness, that she was tempted to just say, "It doesn't matter," and leave. What had she come for? Did she really want to hear what was wrong with her? And so she just sat, aware that the doctor was waiting, while she was unable to form any sort of sentence.

Doctor Jawad leant forward, and gently touched Monica's hand.

"What has happened to you?" she said.

The young woman's eyes were filled with such compassion that Monica was momentarily overcome. It was as though she could see straight past Monica's bravado to the real person inside. Those five words *What has happened to you?* had such a profound effect on her, that she immediately began to sob. They were sobs of relief. It felt like she had been just waiting for someone to notice, for someone who would just stop her and say, "Monica, you're not okay, are you?" but nobody did. Not until now. She felt utter relief. She could tell someone how it had been, how cracked and ragged she truly felt.

With a broken ankle she had had to stop, but with a broken spirit she had been able to go on functioning, looking normal but feeling damaged inside. She couldn't blame people for not noticing, after all she was an actress. A supreme cover up that was now failing, but all she felt now was a sense of release.

Doctor Jawad handed her a box of tissues. "What is making you so upset, Monica?" she said.

Unable to stop the powerful sobs from erupting, she simply shook her head and pressed a tissue to her eyes. "I'm so sorry," she said, in an oddly strangled voice. "I'm so sorry. I'm just being silly."

"Don't be. Whatever it is, I promise you, it isn't silly. If it is making you so upset, it can't be silly. Now, just take a moment to collect yourself and then tell me."

Monica felt as though she would never stop crying. The sadness inside her was forcing its way out and there was nothing she could do about it.

She knew logically that she couldn't sit there crying for the whole of her ten minute consultation but it was so just difficult to explain.

She had buried it so well, as though by ignoring it she could make it go away, but try as she might it had always stayed with her. Maybe it was asleep but it was always there, and now it had woken up and was screaming at her to be let out.

Chapter Thirty Three

"Monica? Can you tell me?" Doctor Jawad was now holding both of her hands and looking into her face with deep concern. "This seems to have been building up for a long time, please try and tell me. Take your time."

Pulling in a huge sob Monica said simply, "My mother died." It was the first time she had used those words. She always referred to it with softer terms like, "passed away," or, "no longer with us." But the truth was Claudette had died. Suddenly and unexpectedly she had left them, and it had been too much to bear.

"Oh, I'm sorry to hear that. When was this, Monica? Recently?"

A strange little laugh bubbled up from Monica's aching throat. "No, no, doctor, it was the Christmas before last. All that time ago and I still can't ......"

"There is no time limit on grief, Monica. What is it that has brought you here today? Has something happened to remind you of your dear mother, perhaps? Something that, maybe took you by surprise?"

"No, I think about her all the time. It's just, lately things have been difficult, I just don't feel...... in control, if that makes sense?"

"You feel anxious?"

"No, I feel terrified, on the brink of a disaster all the time, as though something terrible is about to happen. I'm falling to bloody pieces. I've been pretending it's all okay, but it isn't, it really isn't. I just feel so lost." Another huge wave of sobs rolled out of Monica that forced her to stop speaking.

After a few moments, she unsteadily resumed, "I think I'm going mad. I've started to forget things, things I've known for years and were always there, they simply won't come. It's like there are huge holes in my brain."

"And of course, this is impacting on your life?"

"You could say that. I gave up acting because of it."

"I see."

"And then I did this," said Monica looking down at her cast. "I've been stuck at home, slowly going insane."

"And who is at home with you? Husband? Children?"

"My husband is working away. He's an actor too. I have a cleaner, Patty. She wanted me to come here."

"Because of your memory loss?"

"No, because of the cats." Monica's voice disappeared almost to a whisper as her throat closed in distress.

Doctor Jawad sat back in her chair and sighed softly. "The cats, Monica? Which cats are you talking about?

"No, no, I can't. It's just too silly. I'm sorry, Doctor I'm wasting your time. I really should go, I'm sorry. You must be busy."

Monica began to pull herself up onto the crutch, but the young doctor gestured at her to stay. "Monica," she said, "tell me about your mother."

****

It was the second Christmas Claudette had spent under the same roof as her daughter and son-in-law, and it suited everyone. Trevor and Monica were both working over the festive season and only had Christmas Day off, and Claudette was more than happy to organize everything for them. She always had a childlike joy about her but at Christmas it was magnified and oddly contagious. Even Patty had succumbed and they would sing Christmas carols together: A terrible noise, half in French and half in English, but full of gusto.

To Claudette Christmas was THE celebration of the year. Somehow she had managed to fit a tree into almost every room. There was even a tiny one on top of the microwave, which was surrounded by figures of little skating children that wobbled every time the door was opened or closed. On the front door she had placed a huge holly wreath, which she had ordered especially from their local florist. It was so large it covered the little window in the door and made the hall quite dark, but Claudette was adamant that it stayed, however impractical it was. But that was her nature, pleasure over practicality every time. Life was to be lived and enjoyed.

Everyone had beautifully wrapped presents sitting neatly under the main Christmas tree in the lounge, except for Theodosia's, which were hidden in a drawer in case the temptation became too great. As it was, she had managed to remove most of the baubles and fake candles from the lower branches.

"Choupette, look how much she loves Christmas!" Claudette said, watching the cat daintily hook a wooden tree decoration with her paw and run off with it down the hall.

The pandemonium and panic of the season was all part of the fun as far as Claudette was concerned. Her only solemn moment was on Christmas Eve when she insisted on attending Midnight Mass. She had always done this as long as Monica could remember; she went alone, always wore her mantilla and never spoke a word about it on her return.

About a week before Christmas that particular year, she had had a dizzy spell. It had forced her to sit down on the kitchen chair and wait for it to pass.

"You all right, Claudette?" Patty asked. "Only, I don't like the look of you."

"Well, I cannot help that you do not like my face. It is the only one I have," she had joked, making a little shrug. "It is nothing, I am fine. Just being a little giddy because it is so very nearly Christmas."

But on Christmas Day as Claudette, Trevor and Monica were preparing lunch, she had another odd spell. "It is so hot in here, Cherie and I think maybe the wine has gone to my head. I will just go and sit for a moment. You carry on but do not spoil my food, it must be perfect."

Claudette went into the lounge closely followed by Theodosia, who was hoping for some extra attention. She and 'Grand-mere' had always been the best of friends.

In the kitchen, Trevor and Monica started to sing Christmas carols and shout comments to her in an attempt to keep her involved in the preparations. "Shall I bring you a nice cup of tea, Chef?" Trevor asked Claudette.

"That would be nice, Trevor but only if Sous Chef will allow it. She may need you in the kitchen."

"No, Claudette she's nodding. It seems to be okay, so I'll put the kettle on."

But it was Monica who took the tea to her mother and it was a moment that she would re-live over and over again. At first everything appeared to be normal. Claudette was sitting in her favourite chair and Monica could see part of her tight little bun of white hair above the chair back, so perfect and neat like a ballet dancer's. But then she noticed the cat. Theodosia was sitting on the floor in front of Claudette, her eyes huge and round, her fur slightly raised, and she appeared to be sniffing at her.

When Monica put the tea on the little side table and looked, she saw that her mother's beautiful, apple shaped face had become a horrible distortion of itself. One side looked as though it had been dragged down, with her eyelid drooped, and her mouth was lolling open in a hideous mockery of a smile.

"Mother! Mother, what's happened, what's wrong?"

When Claudette tried to reply her words fell out in a strange tumble of unrecognizable sounds.

"Mother! Trevor!"

Over and over again, Claudette tried to form words but nothing came out except for strange gurgling grunting sounds. She began to rub at her arm which was lying limply across her lap.

"Trevor!" Monica called again.

Her eyes met with her mother's and the terror she saw in them pierced her to the core. It was as though Claudette was frantically struggling to come back to her, as though she was trapped in her suddenly failing body.

Monica instinctively reached out to touch her mother's hand and as she did so, Claudette tried to raise hers, but couldn't. Her unfocused gaze and uncoordinated movement was like a woman slowly drowning in thick, glutinous water.

Trevor came in from the kitchen and crouched down in front of his mother–in–law.

"Claudette, can you hear me? Mon, I think she's having a stroke. I'll ring for an ambulance. You stay with her, just keep talking to her."

Monica took her mother's hand and squeezed it tightly but the hand in hers was now too weak to squeeze back.

As they waited together Claudette seemed to recede into herself, like the flame was slowly being drawn inside. Her eyes became darker and darker until finally, it was though she had been switched off. Or at least that was how Monica saw it in her mind's eye, over and over again. No final jolt or breath, she was just gone.

It wasn't like any death scene she had ever played. The shell that was left behind immediately lost something, the personality was no longer there, all brightness and all the light was gone. Even her mother's habitual forceful expression had left her. That face didn't belong to Claudette. She didn't look at peace, she just looked like a stranger. How many times had Monica knelt on stage, carefully closing the eyes of a fellow actor and declaring them gone? And now this had happened in front of her, so violent and so terrible. It was like nothing she had ever seen before.

She hadn't even said goodbye. She wasn't prepared. Somehow she didn't think it would be like that for Claudette. She had always imagined that there would be plenty of time. Claudette would look pale but beautiful, slowly fading whilst holding court from her bed, issuing directions and instructions until the end. But not this, this was a terrifying attack on her from an unseen enemy, and Monica had been left shattered.

Chapter Thirty Four

Doctor Jawad sat back. "I am so sorry," she said. "That must have been a terrible, terrible shock. And afterwards were you able to grieve?"

Defiantly rubbing away her tears Monica lifted her chin, "I went straight back to work," she said. "It's what we do. You must have heard that, *the Show must go on*. Well, it's true, it really does. Partly for the audience, but for we actors too. It's where we hide. On stage we throw ourselves into the role and shut everything else away."

"But you did grieve? At the funeral? Did you make a little time for yourself to say goodbye?"

"Oh, I played the dignified grief stricken daughter to perfection, Doctor. I wore an impeccable outfit, I said all the right things, but it was just more acting. I couldn't let myself feel it, you see. I couldn't have stood it."

" I see, and then?"

"And then, I just carried on.

"As though nothing had happened? Didn't you talk about your mother? To your husband, perhaps?"

"No, we just got on with our lives. Claudette was a very strong person, she wouldn't have wanted us to do otherwise."

"Tell me, Monica, do you think about your mother often, do you dream about her? Feel angry that she left you, perhaps? Is that why you have tried to shut her out?"

"Shut her out! I haven't shut her out" said Monica distressed. "That isn't it. I came because I can't remember things and because I'm afraid I'm going insane. I probably wouldn't have bothered to come at all but Patty, my cleaner, heard me playing a rather silly game and she thought I'd gone demented."

"A game, Monica?"

"Well, sort of. I made up voices for my cats. It just made me laugh, it was fun. But then she told me about her mentally ill grandfather doing a similar thing and I began to worry."

"But your voices helped you escape from real life. I understand. You are a creative person, you created this little game. I'm not worried at all by that, but I am worried about your other symptoms. I think your mother's death has affected you more than you realize."

"No, Doctor. Really, this is not about my mother."

"But you see, I think it is. All the things you have described to me are all common manifestations of unresolved grief: memory loss; the feeling of dread; sadness; feeling out of control, like you are losing your sanity. Even your accident could be attributed to your state of mind. When I asked you what had happened to you, you told me your mother had died, not that you had lost your memory, or that you had broken your ankle. So please, Monica. Let me help you."

Monica sat for a moment, she was shaking inside. This was not supposed to happen at all. For some reason this young woman had penetrated her armour and made her think about those things which she had locked safely away. She didn't even know why she had told her about her mother's death, and now it was out. There could be no going back.

"Monica, I think you are depressed, and I think you haven't come to terms with your grief. So, this is what I would like to do. Start you off on a course of anti-depressants and arrange for you to see a grief counsellor."

"Anti-depressants!" said Monica.

"Yes, just a low dose. 20 milligrammes. You won't get addicted, I promise. It's just to get you back into a balanced state. I can't guarantee it will work straight away, but they will help."

"I've never been depressed in my life! It's a self-indulgence," Monica spat. "And as for grief counselling, I haven't got time to sit about talking about things like that. My mother has passed away, and having a chat about it won't bring her back."

"No one is saying that it will, but it might help you come to terms with it. And who knows, get you back to work. Back to what you love doing. Isn't that worth trying for?"

"I've retired," said Monica, stubbornly.

"Well then, someone should tell your brain, otherwise it will go on acting, making up voices and games all by itself. Think about it, Monica, please."

Monica hauled herself up on her crutch and with a final withering look said, "Thank you for your time, Doctor Jawad."

It was difficult to make a dignified exit wearing a plaster cast, but Monica felt she had just about managed it. Inside she was boiling up with emotion. It had been a total disaster. The doctor had caught her off guard and she had ended up talking about all sorts of things instead of what she came for. Damn Patty and her stupid family.

The thought of sitting in a room listening to someone spouting psychobabble at her and talking about *closure* filled her with dread. It had never been her way, or Claudette's. They simply carried on, got on with it. But what to tell Patty? She was bound to ask how she'd got on. One word about what had passed and Patty would want to send her off to the therapist, or whatever. Patty had interfered enough and Monica resolved to tell her nothing.

On the way home in the taxi she continued to dwell on the consultation. Of course it was all nonsense. People didn't have counsellors years ago and they survived some terrible things. Her parents had survived a war for goodness' sake. We had all gone soft and she would not be a part of it. It would all pass in time. At least the doctor hadn't mentioned dementia or anything like that.

At the Stonehouse the cats were waiting. As soon as the taxi juddered to a halt, they popped up at the lounge window, opening their mouths in silent greetings. Monica paid the driver and struggled back toward her safe haven.

Inside she slumped down on the settee and threw her crutch down on the floor. There was a note from Patty on the coffee table saying, "Hope it went all right. P." She screwed it up and tossed it down to an eager Ghilly who then dribbled it across the floor before flicking it high into the air.

Had she *got on all right?* No, she bloody well hadn't. Some young woman had decided she was depressed and couldn't handle her mother's death. It was ridiculous. What could she know about anything, she looked fresh from medical school. They are all told to spout this stuff about trauma and issues nowadays. They were making everyone neurotic.

She had faced up to Claudette's death in her own way. She knew she had gone. She was there when she died, so how could the doctor say she had unresolved grief? If anyone knew she had gone, it was Monica.

She stretched over and took out an old photo album from the drawer beside her. It contained pictures of Claudette: holidays, birthdays, happy times. She hadn't looked at it for a long time.

As she placed it on her lap, Theodosia jumped up and sat squarely on top of it and looked deep into Monica's eyes. "Reee-ow," she said.

"What's the matter, darling. Don't you think I'm up to it? Well, this old stick is a tough one. Come on, off you get."

Monica slid her finger inside the cover and opened the album. The very first picture was of Claudette as a young woman, jet black hair piled up in a loose bun and a bright dauntless look shining from her dark eyes. This was a young woman who lived with a fierce energy inside her, as though she couldn't wait for the future to come to her. It was a look she never lost.

Monica turned the page. There was a picture of her mother and father on holiday, walking along some unknown pier, dressed in dark rain coats. It was in black and white but somehow Claudette shone out from the drab surroundings.

Theodosia placed an elegant paw on the page and pressed.

"Stop it, I'm trying to look at Grand-mere," she said. On the next page Monica caught sight of herself, at three or maybe four years old, holding her mother's hand as they walked in a sunny garden. In the background, a large Siamese cat was watching them with half closed eyes.

Monica touched the page. She could remember the feeling of her mother's hand in hers, the sun and the bright flowers in the borders. And then she drew in a huge choking breath that then it let itself back out again in short jagged sobs. "Mother," she said.

Chapter Thirty Five

It had been six weeks since Monica had visited Doctor Jawad and had so completely broken down. It wasn't so much that she had given in, it was more that the thin thread that had been holding her together had finally snapped.

Summer had started to show itself in patches of the garden and the nights were getting lighter. It was as though both she and the seasons had been through a dark time and were now emerging together.

Patty had been very self-righteous and had gone about wearing her "I knew this would happen" face, but she seemed content to keep her smugness to herself and in a rare show of sentiment, Patty had sent her a card with an inspirational phrase and a sunflower on it. It said,

This is not about weakness, it is about having tried to be strong for far too long.

Usually Monica hated such trite little homilies, but she felt there was more than a grain of truth in it. She had tried to be strong for too long. How could she expect to lose someone like Claudette and just carry on? It just wasn't possible and she knew that now.

Trevor was now managing to come home on a regular basis. That first evening when she had called him full of tears and pain, still holding the photo album to her chest, he had driven straight home after the show. They had hardly spoken that night. Trevor had just held her while she sobbed.

But it was the beginning of healing, or so her counsellor, Helen, had told her. The beginning of the grief process. Monica had turned up for her sessions as meekly as a lamb, no longer resisting help, simply determined to feel better.

Her cast had finally been removed too and she expected to feel euphoric but instead she had weeks of painful physiotherapy ahead of her. It was as though she had been broken into very small pieces like Humpty Dumpty and now they were putting her back together again.

But at least she had begun to feel lighter inside, not brittle and dark any more. Her face didn't feel tight now, just old and battle scarred. But as Helen said, it would take time. Her moth brain still haunted her, things still disappeared from her mind just when she needed them, but perhaps she had to accept it for the time being. It would eventually come back, she was told, but for now she just needed to be patient.

The cats had become her nurses. It was as though they knew they were needed. One or both were with her constantly and at night they slept, one on either side of her pillow. If she awoke with a strange sense of panic that sometimes struck her, two sets of moon diamond eyes shone from the darkness, reassuring her that all was well.

She was still apt to put voices to them, it was so hard to resist.

"What are you doing now, King of The Kilt People?"

"Just playing with this wee thing I found in the kitchen. It's a great smelly little thing with a tail."

"That, is an Earl Grey Tea bag, moron!"

Or the day Ghilly got a tissue box stuck on his head and hurtled about the house screaming that he had been attacked.

"It's got me, it was like a Venus fly trap! I just was having a wee look at it and now it's on me......Get it off! Get It off."

"I'd leave it on, if I were you. It's a great improvement."

Monica didn't worry about it now. She understood it; it was just her brain acting. She had done it for so long, she just couldn't expect to turn it off. It would have been like asking a dancer not to tap her feet when she heard music playing.

As time moved on it became harder to place herself back in the state of mind she had been in. And every day she moved further away, and every day she felt a little more calm.

Claudette had been the most wonderful mother and she had been taken away in the most brutal way, but she would not have wanted to take Monica with her. Monica was her legacy and she needed drink in every drop of life, like Claudette had done.

One summer morning, as Patty was droning unmusically to herself as she went about her work, she suddenly announced to Monica,

"I thought of you last night. I were watching a programme about animation, kiddies cartoons and alike and there was this actor, Antonio summat or another, Spanish most probably, and he were doing the voice for a cat."

"Really? Was it a Siamese?"

"No, it were wearing a hat. Anyway, he were having a grand time, acting it all out….. But here's the thing, he had his script in front of him on a lectern thing."

"Hmmm?" said Monica, not quite sure what this was all about.

"Well, it's only doing what you were doing with them cats, only not as barmy and he were getting paid. I reckon you'd be good at that, and you wouldn't have to remember owt."

"Voice over work!" said Monica, horrified.

"Well, I don't know what they call it, but if you say so. Looked right up your street."

Monica was just about to say, *I am a trained actress,* when she stopped. She had been feeling so restless lately and what good is being a trained actress if you don't act. When she had started out and needed to take very small roles, Claudette had always told her, "Acting is acting." Wasn't that still true? Didn't she miss it?

Having received no response Patty said, "Well, you can suit yourself, of course, but I just thought I'd mention it."

"Thank you, Patty," said Monica. "Really, thank you for thinking about me."

And her 'thank you' was a sincere one. Patty had thought of her many times over the last few months. She had in fact been a loyal if slightly odd friend to Monica. She had the biggest, kindest heart imaginable, it was just wrapped up in a slightly dour exterior. Far from seeing her as dull and inferior any more, Monica now felt real affection for her and unlikely though it seemed, they had become friends.

Monica's mind returned to Patty's suggestion. Clara had mentioned voiceover work several times. Just suppose it was a way back, just suppose the show really could go on again? Claudette had always told her that there is always an answer. Maybe this was it.

She'd do it, she decided....and she'd make a bloody good job of it!

An ominous thump from upstairs, followed by a wild skittering of paws disturbed Monica's thoughts. Ghilly and Theodosia entered the lounge at full pelt, narrowly avoiding crashing into the coffee table. Ghilly's ears were back and his eyes had a wild look about them.

"Get her off me!" he wailed. *"I only said she had the figure of an athlete. It was a compliment"*

"You said a weightlifter, sporran face!"